The
Minotaur Medallion

Bill K. Underwood

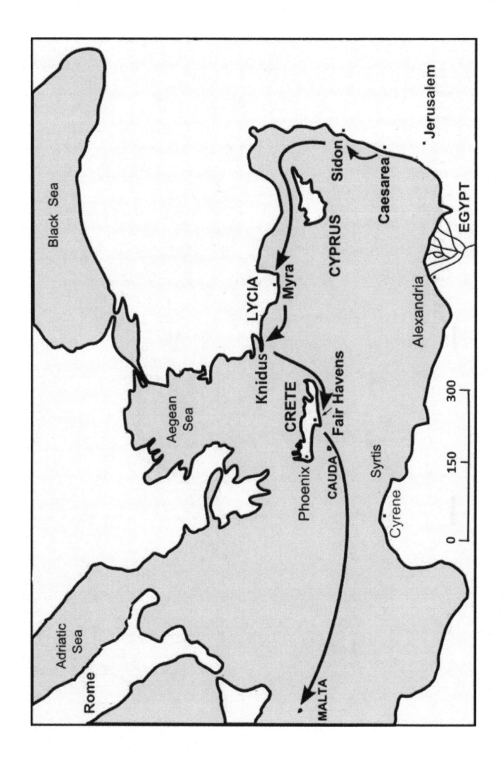

St. Paul's Bay, Malta

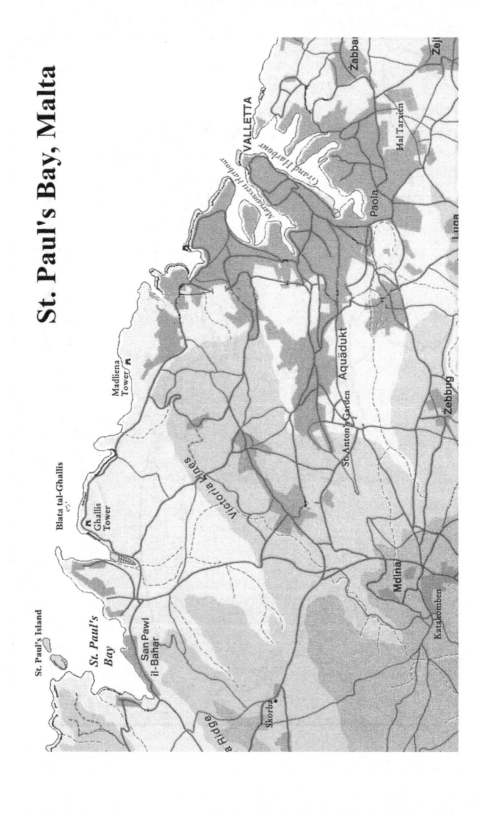

CHAPTER 1

WHEN I ROLLED BACKWARD off the side of the boat, the difference was instantly obvious. It was like diving into a martini. If there'd been an olive on the bottom I probably could have seen it.

It made me wonder what kind of muck I'd been swimming in over the past few weeks, when I could barely see to the end of my arm. Actually, I guess I didn't want to think too much about that. Surely it was just tourists' sunblock and hand cream that clouded the water of Saint Paul's Bay where I had been swimming; not oil spills, or bilge water from boats, or worse...

In fairness, the European version of *The Weather Channel* on the TV in my hotel room had been reporting for most of the last two weeks that there was a fierce storm in the eastern Mediterranean. Though we hadn't seen the storm here, we'd seen the effects. The surfers loved it. And it was probably the roiling surf as much as the pollution that was responsible for the poor visibility I'd been struggling with since I arrived.

But I was now diving about a hundred yards off a beach roughly a half mile south of Saint Paul's Bay, on the east coast of Malta. Malta is a flyspeck of an island about 500 miles south of Italy, smack in the middle of the shipping lanes between Europe and Africa. It was a beautiful beach, but if it had a name, I didn't know what it was. There was no bay at all to protect this spot from the Med, but there was a pile of rocks jutting from the sea just north of me; and what looked like some sort of a shoal or reef connecting the shore to the rocks just beneath the water. A ship lost in the dark might hear the surf hitting those rocks and assume they were closer to land than they actually were. The shoal water behind the rock-pile was clearly visible now, in broad daylight. But in bad weather or at night, that shoal would be a deadly menace to an unsuspecting sailor.

There were no other boats here, unlike the crowded harbor at Saint Paul's Bay. Coming south from Saint Paul's Bay to this nameless beach I'd passed another bay which did have a name, but not one I could pronounce. That bay was as crowded with boats as its shoreline was with condominiums. By contrast, the shoreline here was nearly uninhabited. From the boat I could see a coast road at the top of an undeveloped beach fringed by the grays and greens of sea grass and wild shrubs, the occasional car zipping past from Saint Paul's Bay to points south. A minaret due west of where my boat was anchored indicated a Muslim mosque on a low hill above the road, and I was pretty sure I'd seen someone up there in the tower occasionally watching my progress. I suppose it was rare to see someone diving here.

There was a house a few hundred yards north of the mosque, and another one about a quarter of a mile south. The northern one was a brand new monstrosity straight out of the *Salvador Dali* school of architecture. The one to the south was more traditional, though somewhat the worse for wear. It looked like it had been around for centuries and was gradually merging right into the landscape itself.

6

Several miles to the south was some sort of amusement park. Other than those, and the occasional car buzzing past on the coastal road, I had the coast to myself.

I'd come to Malta because of its biblical connection. I guess you could call me an armchair archaeologist, if there is such a thing. I subscribed to *Biblical Archaeology Review* and similar magazines and studied them diligently, even though I usually disagreed with the conclusions their decidedly *non*-biblical authors came to. (Why would someone become a "biblical" archaeologist if they don't believe the Bible? Why not be a Navajo archaeologist? For that matter, why not be a landscaper? You're still playing in the dirt all day, and the pay is better.)

Anyway, in the section of the Bible called *Acts of the Apostles,* or just *Acts* for short, there's an account of the apostle Paul being taken as a prisoner on board a ship bound for Rome that wrecked on the coast of a small island the Greek text refers to as *Melita*. The Maltese believe the story, which is why they have a town named Saint Paul's Bay. And most scholars agree the biblical *Melita* is present-day Malta. But there has been no archaeological evidence found on Malta that definitively proves the story.

So when my business finally reached a point where I could take a real vacation without fearing it would collapse in my absence, I decided Malta would be a great place to spend a month or two. Hence the two fruitless weeks of diving in the murky waters of Saint Paul's Bay.

'Fruitless' may not be the right word. Before leaving Phoenix I'd purchased a Garrett "Sea Hunter," a state-of-the-art underwater metal detector that claimed to be waterproof down to three hundred feet, and while I had no plans to test it to that depth it clearly worked well. So far I'd found three cameras, several pairs of sunglasses, a couple watches, over a dozen wedding rings, and an artificial leg. (How does a person lose an artificial leg?) That haul alone – not including the leg – would cover all my dive rental fees and most of my hotel bill. My new best friend Anthony, the proprietor of the dive shop where I'd rented what gear I hadn't been able to bring on the plane, was trying to find the owner of the leg. No doubt he would ask for a reward.

I'd also found some stuff that I guess you could call

archaeological, just not the right vintage. I'd dug up some brass fittings that were familiar to Anthony; he'd identified them as coming from a WWII era British warship. I'd also come up with a sharp hunk of metal that turned out to be a boarding pike off of a French ship of the Napoleonic era. Anthony had a 'very good friend,' a collector of nautical antiques, who was willing to pay enough for those items to cover my expenses for another week, maybe two.

Everyone, it seemed, was Anthony's 'very good friend.' Anthony was the classic image of a jolly grandfather: In his sixties, large around the middle and bald on top. He laughed easily, and only if you watched very closely did you notice that his eyes weren't always laughing when the rest of him was.

My best find so far was a short curved sword or dagger, mostly rusted but with the handle surprisingly intact. The handle was carved from some kind of wood neither of us could identify, and both the handle and the back half of the blade were overlaid with gold. Anthony was certain it was a Saracen *kilij*, probably dropped as the Saracens – Muslims, we call them today – were being routed by the Catholics during the Siege of Malta on Tuesday, September 11, 1565. He'd looked it up on the internet and made me an offer that would have kept me in both hotel and dive rentals for two, maybe three additional weeks.

Instead of accepting I had pointed behind him and asked, "That room in back with the bed, does anyone use it?"

He was surprised – perhaps embarrassed? – that I was asking about it. "Oh that. I sleep there sometimes when I work late, or when my wife is unhappy with me," he answered. "Why?"

"Suppose you stay on your wife's good side and let me move out of my hotel into your back room?"

"No, David, that room is a mess! I couldn't put you in there, my friend. I would be a terrible host!"

"Anthony, I'm a bachelor. I don't care what the room looks like as long as the bed's comfortable and the shower works."

"Well, I suppose something could be arranged, if that's what you want." He thought for a bit. "Um, how much would you be willing to pay for the room?"

"Here's what I was thinking. Give me the room and unlimited

use of the dive boat and all the gear I need for, say, eight more weeks, and I'll give you the dagger or *kilij* or whatever it's called."

"An excellent idea, David! But, perhaps... four weeks... would be closer to the value of this rusty dagger?"

He looked at me appraisingly. I knew what he was seeing: a young guy of average height, curly brown hair bleached to blonde by the Phoenix sunshine and beginning to thin. My slim frame gave no indication of muscles, but if he looked closely in my blue eyes he had to see the same calculating determination I saw in his. My business hadn't become a success by accident.

I could tell he wasn't going to let go of the *kilij* in spite of the rust. I was sure that in no time it would have a place of prominence in his display case. He'd use it to convince prospective customers of how rich they would get if they rented equipment from him.

While I was having a lot of fun, I didn't really plan to stay on vacation for two more months; but I knew he'd want to haggle.

"So, six weeks, then?" I asked.

He stuck out his hand. "My wife will clean it out today and you can move in tomorrow."

It was a good deal for both of us. Six more weeks at the Hotel would cost a fortune, and the *kilij* was probably worth a similar fortune, so we were even. More than that, though, I was starting to get into the underwater salvage thing and I sure wasn't ready to go back to Phoenix just yet.

***

THE NEXT DAY, I FOUND his wife had really gone out of her way to make the little room hospitable, installing curtains, a microwave and a small TV. She'd also scrubbed the toilet and shower, though they had been ignored almost too long to save. It didn't matter. I liked the idea that I was staying almost free in an idyllic spot most tourists paid thousands to visit.

But I was really fixated on finding something, anything, from the first century in the water around Saint Paul's Bay. I expressed my disappointment to Anthony.

"But what do you expect, my friend?" Anthony commiserated.

"It would be amazing if anything lasted underwater that long. And anything that did – well, do you think you're the first person to look?" He waved expansively at the bay visible out of the back side of his shop, where we could see hundreds of tourists swimming, snorkeling, jet-skiing, or just bobbing in the water. "Even with your fancy metal finder?" He had a point.

Still, I had hoped. I had walked through the local museum; and I'd paid for admission to a diorama about the Pauline shipwreck set up for tourists at one of the high-end resorts. Both had displays explaining the wreck of the unnamed ship which had stranded the apostle Paul and two hundred seventy-five other people on Malta, but neither display contained a single first century artifact.

On the evening of my sixteenth day in Malta, I decided to re-read the account in the book of Acts to see if there were any clues there that I'd missed. And there was one, a big one, that jumped out at me.

And that was why I was now diving in a different place.

CHAPTER 2

"YOU ARE ASKING ME to play nursemaid to a bunch of prisoners? Do I need to explain to you the duties of a centurion?"

"My apologies, my lord Julius," the prefect said. "I mean you no disrespect." He gestured to the gold-encrusted blue glass phalera displaying the portrait of Caesar Augustus which dangled, with several other badges of honor, from Julius' breastplate. "Your exploits with the Augustus band are legendary!"

Smarmy rodent, thought Julius. Jumped-up jailer. Petty bureaucratic weasel...

Julius was a tall man made more imposing by his erect carriage. His ice blue eyes were topped by black hair going to gray, cut short. A scar disfigured the left side of what was otherwise a handsome face with a strong, aquiline nose. It took little imagination to picture him taking on, and defeating, dozens if not hundreds of attackers.

The smarmy rodent quickly went on.

"I would never normally ask someone of your acclaimed personage to take on such a menial task," though both men knew that was exactly what he was doing. "But since you are travelling to Rome anyway, and you have a bodyguard of six, I thought perhaps you could simply assign one of your guards to watch these few prisoners."

"They are called my bodyguards for a reason," said Julius. "They guard *me*. I do not need them distracted by a bunch of criminals."

The prefect was frantic to win this one. If he sent some of his men to Rome as prisoner escorts this late in the year he wouldn't get them back until spring. They would have a nice Roman holiday while their salaries would continue to be deducted from his budget. And probably their expenses.

"Then this is most fortuitous!" the prefect gushed. "These are not criminals, not in the usual sense, at least not all of them... One is only a deserter from the Praetorian Guard..." a scowl from Julius made the prefect decide to change tack. He hurried on.

"And one hasn't even been convicted of anything! He's simply caught in the middle of some Jewish dispute."

In spite of himself, Julius couldn't help asking, "Why would he be going to Rome because of a Jewish dispute?"

"He is a Roman citizen. Well, all three of them are Roman citizens. The two charged with crimes both stood on their citizenship and appealed to Caesar. And, of course the Praetorian can't be punished by anyone but Nero. So, His Excellency the governor is sending them to Rome. And I'm shorthanded and have no guards to spare." The prefect was actually wringing his hands.

Another moment and he'll be kissing the hem of my tunic, thought Julius. But mention of Governor Festus had captured Julius' attention for another reason.

"This Roman Jew... he wouldn't by any chance be named Paul?"

"I don't know, let me look... well, he's listed as Saul Paulus of Tarsus, so I suppose he might be called Paul. Why, do you know him?"

"I've never met the man," said Julius. "But King Agrippa and I were guests of Governor Festus..." at this the prefect quailed even more obsequiously than he had been, to think he was asking a favor of someone who was a friend of both the

12

Roman governor and the Judean king. "Festus invited us to sit in when Paul made his defense. The man presented a powerful argument. I found him very, er, persuasive. So did the king, for that matter."

"Wonderful!" said the prefect. "This is most propitious. The gods are smiling on you. You will have someone with whom you can pass the time on your voyage to Rome. And this Paul has two servants with him, so he'll make no work for your guards at all."

In the end, Julius grudgingly agreed. He hated giving the prefect the satisfaction, but the last argument had hit its mark. His previous sea voyages had proven boring beyond belief. His guards, though his constant companions, were not chosen for their conversational skills. The only dialogue he ever heard from them began and ended with "Yes, sir, absolutely, sir, right away, sir." And sea captains, though widely travelled, were not much better. Under the Roman system, as soon as Julius stepped on board a ship he became the senior officer, and captains tended to avoid conversation with him except to ask for orders.

From what Julius had heard, Paul was nearly as well travelled as any sea captain. And he'd proven before Festus and Agrippa that he wasn't afraid to speak his mind. Julius found he was actually looking forward to the trip that, moments before, he'd been viewing with resignation.

Almost as an afterthought Julius asked, "What about the third one?"

"Third one? Third what, my lord?" the prefect asked.

"You said there were three prisoners."

"Oh! Yes, that. Well, he has been charged with defrauding widows, and, um, murder. But he appealed, so, he may not be..."

Julius just growled and left the guardroom.

**

A CHAIN RAN FROM the right wrist of Demetrius, defrauder of widows and possible murderer, to the belt of a soldier of Julius' bodyguard, a huge man named Otho, whose brow gave the appearance of someone struggling to think deeply. The appearance was deceiving. Before they had travelled a hundred paces, Otho discovered his loculus was gone. He stopped and, over the prisoner's objections, found it tucked under Demetrius' girdle. Not satisfied with its return he inspected the contents; several coins were missing. He reached for Demetrius.

"No! It wasn't me!" Demetrius loudly proclaimed. "Someone framed me! I just found it on the ground, I haven't even opened it!"

Displaying the qualities that had gotten him his position as one of Julius' guards Otho didn't waste time arguing. He simply bent over and grabbed Demetrius by one of his ankles and pulled upward. Demetrius' head bounced off the ground as he screamed and tried to kick his leg free, but Otho's grip was like iron. He caught Demetrius' other leg and held the man virtually upside-down. After a few shakes, the missing coins began to appear.

The band of twelve, a centurion, six Roman soldiers, three prisoners, and the two men with Paul – Julius was surprised to discover they were not, in fact, Paul's servants but his friends, a physician named Luke and a Macedonian named Aristarchus – made their way to the artificial harbor formed by a seawall that jutted out from the rocky coast of Caesarea.

The seawall ran west from the coast a few stadia then turned sharply north. A second seawall extended from the coast a short distance to the north of the first and reached almost to meet the first, leaving only a north-facing gap through which ships entered and exited the harbor. The south seawall had sluice gates built into it that were occasionally opened so that the north-bound coastal current would clear out the spoiled freight, trash, dead dogs, and other detritus that built up in the harbor. Unfortunately, judging by the smell, the sluice gates had not been opened for some time.

The top of the seawall was paved and crowded with emporiums and warehouses of every description. It thronged with merchants hawking their wares, slaves shopping for exotic goods for their households, sailors on leave, and travelers seeking passage to other ports. The small protected space created by the seawall was packed with dozens of small ships. But Julius could find no ships bound for Rome.

After a frustrating morning traipsing around the harbor, Julius finally signed a chit for passage on board a small vessel that would take them north to Myra where, Julius hoped, he might still find a Rome-bound ship. The captain was obviously irritated by it, knowing it would be months, if ever, before he turned the chit into coin, but he didn't dare refuse the centurion.

The captain gruffly informed him, "I can't feed all of you. Make sure you bring enough food for two weeks."

"Two weeks? To get to Myra?"

"We aren't going straight to Myra," the captain explained. "This is a *coaster*, we'll be making several stops along the *coast*. We should be in Sidon tomorrow, if the wind favors us. I have business to attend to there for a few days. When I'm finished with that we'll make for… well, it doesn't matter. Several stops, then Myra. If you need to get to Myra sooner, you can probably find some other coaster…"

"I'm sure this will be fine. But why food for two weeks if we're stopping every day?"

"I never trust the wind this time of year. We could be blown out to sea faster than, well, faster than my men can get the sail down."

CHAPTER
3

IF IT WEREN'T FOR THE BLEEP of the metal detector I'd have dismissed it as a rock. When the detector sounded off I had shifted about twelve inches of sand before I saw the round, brown blob. I waved the magic wand over it a couple more times, and the bleep said it was definitely metal. Only when I dug it out and brought it close to my mask could I see faint manmade markings on the small object lying in my palm. I dropped it into my collection bag.

So far, this new spot had yielded some beer cans, some huge nails that looked pretty old, and a piece of hardware (junk would probably be a better term) that I couldn't identify. It all went in my bag, even the trash.

After re-reading Acts chapter twenty-seven, I'd bounced my new theory off Anthony.

"There's no beach." I had said, pointing out his back window at the bay.

"True enough, my friend. But it has been two thousand years. There are no vipers on Malta, either; at least, that's what we claim when there are tourists within earshot. Yet Paul was bitten by a viper. Do we discount the whole island?"

"The vipers at least left skeletons."

Anthony sighed. "Beaches don't leave skeletons. The beach, like the vipers, may have simply gone away with the passage of time."

"Yes, but... Look," I had pointed out. "The account says first, in the dark, they sensed they were nearing land. How would they have guessed that – by hearing waves crashing, right?"

"Most likely, yes. They could have smelled land..."

"The wind was behind them."

"True. So it is more likely what is meant is that they heard or perhaps saw the surf hitting either Trunciera Point on the south of the entrance to the bay, or Saint Paul's Islands north of the bay."

"Right, that's always been the theory. And the account says when they heard that or sensed it or whatever, they dropped a lead line and found twenty fathoms. And then it shoaled to fifteen fathoms and they dropped some anchors by the stern. Which makes sense because no one is going to try to land on a strange beach at night in a storm."

"Precisely." Anthony had patiently rewarded me with a smile and a nod as if he were a teacher and I his rather dimwitted student. He had grown up with the Bible story ingrained in him like Americans grow up hearing about George Washington chopping down a cherry tree.

I'd pressed on. "And, the next day, they saw a beach and decided to try to ground the ship there, right?"

This time Anthony had merely nodded his agreement.

"So, Anthony: even if there was a beach back then over there – "I had pointed west to the head of Saint Paul's Bay. "– could you see it if you were on a boat anchored at the fifteen fathom line over there?" I had then pointed east, toward the ocean beyond Saint Paul's Island that we both knew couldn't be seen from his dive shop.

"Hmm. So, perhaps they landed on the point itself, or one of the islands?"

"Doesn't fit," I'd replied. "There's no beach on the point."

"There may have..."

"There may have been a beach two thousand years ago, yes. But there also is no shoal between the point and the fifteen fathom line for them to wreck on. Are we to believe both the beach and the shoal disappeared?"

"Perhaps on one of the islands themselves."

"If they landed on one of the islands, how would the

17

inhabitants of Malta ever have found them? Two hundred seventy-six people? They'd have starved out there."

Anthony had paused and frowned at that. "So, what are you suggesting, my friend? Are we going to have to rename our town?"

"Nothing so drastic. I came here because of the name. I think the town is named for Paul because this is *approximately* the right place, just not *exactly* the right place. Let's assume there was a town here in the first century; suppose it was the only town for miles. If Paul's ship ended up a mile or two north or south of here, they would still have brought the survivors to the town, right?"

"Certainly."

"And of course there's no reason to believe they changed the name of the town at the time. But it does make sense that their descendants, hearing the story passed down about saving the people from Paul's ship, might have changed the name. That's why I'm staying close to the bay. If Paul's wreck happened in Saint Thomas bay down south of Valetta where they found those first century anchors a few years ago, doesn't it seem like they would have name it for Paul instead of Saint Thomas? Wouldn't the traditional stories about the wreck be there instead of here?"

Anthony had nodded. "I've never believed those stories about the anchors in Saint Thomas. So, where will you start, north or south?"

"Let me show you." I'd pulled up Google Earth on my laptop and zoomed in on Saint Paul's bay, then panned a bit south. "Here's a beach. And here," I pointed to the offshore rocks, "is something that sailors could hear surf hitting on a dark stormy night. And," widening the Google view a bit, "sailors on a ship anchored at the fifteen fathom line here would also be able to see a beach: this beach."

He'd nodded and rattled off something that sounded like 'blast a giraffe.' "So this will be your new hunting ground?"

"It's worth a shot."

He had poked at the screen. "Why not Melliena Bay?" His gnarled finger was pointing north of Saint Paul's Bay.

"No shoal. No sandbar. If they'd seen that beach and decided to beach their ship there, it seems like they would have succeeded. Correct me if I'm wrong, but it doesn't look like there's anything there that would have unexpectedly wrecked the ship before it hit the beach."

Anthony didn't need to consult a sailing chart. "No, you're right. The bottom of Melliena Bay is a gradual rise all the way from the open sea to the beach. So, you go south?"

"I go south," I had told him.

"Well," he had said. "You will need help. Diving alone in the bay out back here with hundreds of tourists around is one thing, but you certainly can't dive alone so far from town. Let me call my grandson." I expected him to head for the phone, but instead he stuck his head out the front door. "Vito!"

Vito had come in shyly, like he was afraid he was in trouble. He was about 12, thin as a stick, an unruly mass of black curls topping his head, his skin dark from spending most of his days shirtless and sunscreen-less.

"He's a diver?" I asked skeptically.

"Like a fish, my friend."

I'd met Vito a couple times already, I just hadn't realized he was Anthony's grandson. I thought he was one of the dozens of street urchins that were always hanging around tourists. He'd offered to help on a couple of my previous dives in Saint Paul's Bay ("Tourist man need help? Five Euro!") but I'd always declined the help, assuming he was just another beggar.

"Vito, Mr. Connor is going to dive the beach at..." It still sounded like "blast a giraffe." Unless I became a native of Malta I'd never be able to pronounce that mishmash of syllables correctly. "He'll need a diving buddy in an isolated spot like that. You go with him."

"Ok, Papa." Vito had turned to me with a wide grin and held out his hand. "Ten Euro, tourist man!"

***

IT ACTUALLY WAS MUCH EASIER with Vito along. Since he'd been diving almost daily since he could walk while I only dove three or four times a year, he was a far more accomplished diver than I. When I was making shallow dives – forty to fifty feet – he generally didn't dive with me; but he was always in the water when I was, wearing a mask and snorkel and keeping a close eye on me. And when I surfaced

19

beside the boat his surprisingly strong arms helped lift my diving harness and tank, making it easier to climb aboard.

Before I had even toweled off, he was rummaging through the dive bag. I barely caught his arm in time to prevent him throwing the beer cans back overboard.

"Why do you want to save that junk?" he asked.

"Amazing how your English has improved."

"My grandfather insists I learn right English."

"Proper English."

"Proper English, right. But the tourists want to believe they are in a foreign country, so pidgin works best for them," he said with the ever-present grin. "But, why you keeping the junk?"

"I know it's junk, but it's junk I'd rather not keep finding. Think of it this way: we're helping clean up the ocean. Keep the beer cans. When you have two pounds of them, you can take them to the recycle center and trade them for a Euro."

Back at the dive shop I showed Anthony my haul. He raised an eyebrow at the beer cans, but Vito rattled off something in Maltese, and Anthony sent him to fetch a barrel to begin his beer can collection. See, I can be green.

Out of the water, the spikes now took on distinguishing features. Anthony began separating them.

"These aren't anything; they look like, I don't know, railroad spikes, maybe," he said, pushing a half dozen aside. "Probably ballast lost from some old sailing ship. But these," he picked up two others. "These are hand forged bronze, my friend. I doubt if they have enough unique characteristics to identify their age or use, but I'm no expert. You may want to take them to the museum. Same with this, whatever it is." The unidentifiable hunk of metal looked like a large thimble, a little over a foot long, with ears protruding from each side. It too was clearly bronze, though neither Anthony nor I could figure out what it was.

Lastly, he picked up the small object I'd almost mistaken for a rock. He pulled a plastic pan from under the counter and half-filled it with fresh water, then came up with a bottle of vinegar and poured in a healthy dose. He immersed the object in the pan and began scrubbing at it with a toothbrush. While he was doing this, a priest

20

walked in.

Anthony quickly wiped his hands on a towel and hurried over to hug the priest and kiss him on both cheeks.

"David, allow me to introduce my good friend Father Jim. He is a diver, too! Father, this is my good friend David Connor from Phoenix, America."

"Glad to meet you, Jim," I said, sticking out my hand.

"It's *Father* Jim," he coolly replied.

There was a trace of British but it sounded unreal, like an American playing around with an English accent. He was a soft-looking man with a red face and somewhat blurry features, dressed in a black robe. He had the look of someone whose red face was probably permanent. He smelled vaguely of oranges.

"Oh," I said, "Sorry, I'm not Catholic. Besides, I'm sure I don't have to tell you what Matthew 23:9 says do I, Jim?" I smiled and patted his shoulder to try to soften the blow to his pride, but I doubt if it helped.

He turned away from me and took Anthony aside for a whispered conversation. I continued scrubbing at the piece of metal soaking in the water and vinegar bath. Slowly, a picture began to emerge.

"Anthony, you need to see this!" I called.

He and the priest hurried over.

"Check this out. It looks like a bull, maybe, with a couple circles around it. Could it be a coin? It's kind of big." I handed it to Anthony while I went to my room to retrieve my camera.

When I came back Anthony was holding it up next to the priest's pendant, a heavy silver cross on a chain that dangled nearly to his waist. Not quite a Maltese cross, more of a traditional cross but with an overlaid circle. The piece with the bull's head was roughly the same size, and it stood out nicely against the black background of the priest's cassock.

"Smile!" I snapped a couple pictures. 'Father' Jim looked like he'd swallowed a toad. Clearly he and I were never going to be pals, but I'd grabbed the shot because I liked the size comparison. "Maybe if I post it on Facebook someone will be able to tell me what it is."

"I was comparing it to Father Jim's cross because of this," said

Anthony, pointing to the edge of the disc. I could see two small irregularities where he was pointing. "I believe there used to be a loop here attaching it to a chain, to wear it around one's neck, do you see? As Father Jim wears his."

"Seems reasonable, but I have no idea."

During this exchange the priest had waved to Anthony and left the shop without so much as a glance or nod at me, probably in a hurry to get away from the heretic who refused to call him 'Father.'

"I apologize for Father Jim," Anthony said. "He was asking about using the back room tonight, and was disappointed when I told him I'd rented it to you."

"What use would a priest have for your back room?" I asked, though I suspected what the answer would be. Anthony gave me a look, and shook his head.

"I've never asked him who he brings here," said Anthony. "I don't imagine being celibate is easy. None of us are perfect..."

I wasn't going to touch that one. No one forced him to take a vow of celibacy, but I held my peace. Anthony too was ready to change the subject.

"I don't know if Facebook is going to be much help with these things. Why don't you take everything to the museum? If we are right about these things being truly ancient, perhaps they will trade you some information for some of the spikes?"

***

I WAS FAMILIAR WITH the displays of the museum, but not the back offices. I approached a young man at the main desk. He had a ring through his eyebrow and a tattoo of a skull on the side of his neck. He wore a bored expression and a name tag with something I could not read (probably the Maltese equivalent of "Hello, my name is...") above the name 'Luca.'

"Good morning, Luca. Is there someone I can see to get some information about these?" I laid the spikes and the thimble-shaped piece of hardware on the desk in front of him.

Luca picked up the chunk of bronze. "That looks old," he advised me. "What is it?" Big help, Luca.

22

"Perhaps there is someone here who would have more information about it?" I prompted as tactfully as I could.

He poked a button on the phone and spoke to someone in Maltese for a bit, then sat down and turned the hunk of metal over in his hands while we waited.

"You think it's gold?" he asked.

"No. I don't think gold turns black like that. Besides, if I had a chunk of gold that size I'd be a millionaire. It's probably bronze." He appeared to lose interest.

After a couple minutes a matronly woman came out and introduced herself as what sounded like 'Elvis,' and escorted me back to her office. There was a sign on her desk that read 'Elspeth Cachia.'

I laid out my bits of metal. She looked at the bronze items, then looked at me questioningly. "From the sea? From here, from Malta?" she asked.

"Yes, I found them right near here, in about 30 feet of water, just off the beach."

"I've seen many of these bronze spikes," she said. "They were used from ancient times right up until a few hundred years ago, to attach the, how do you call it, the planks, the siding? The boards on the side and bottom of boats, attach them to the ribs. Even after iron spikes became common on land, bronze was still used for ships because of the water, the rust, you understand?"

I did. "What about this?" I pointed to the piece that looked like a thimble with ears.

She began rummaging through the books and papers on an overcrowded table behind her desk. She finally came up with an auction catalog.

"I remember a picture," she began, flipping pages. "Here it is." She opened a drawer and took out a small tape measure and held it against the old metal piece in several directions.

"Yours is smaller. But if you discount the encrustations," she said, "It's almost exactly the same shape. The description in the catalog calls it 'A foremast cap with Egyptian decoration and eyelets for rope handling.' These protrusions might be eyelets once all the scale is removed. Until yours is restored there's no way to tell if there is some decoration under there. The one in the catalog is described as

23

first century B.C."

I was stunned. The ship Paul was on was a grain carrier from Alexandria, Egypt, less than 200 years newer than the one in the catalog. Could it be I'd found it already?

Elvis, I mean Elspeth, immediately burst my bubble. "Of course, the auction people based their description on where it was found, casting marks, and especially on the design motif, details we cannot see on yours. Until we do some serious cleaning we won't know what we have. But based on the amount of buildup, I think it's safe to say its age is-" I waited, holding my breath... "– well, very old, at least a thousand years."

Well, that slowed me down. Big difference between dating something less than two hundred years from Paul's wreck, and a thousand years later. But perhaps after it was cleaned up we would know more.

Now for the bull-headed coin or charm thing. I laid it on her desk. "Any ideas about this?"

She rubbed it with her fingers, pulled out a magnifying glass and looked at both sides. She finally handed it back to me. "No, sorry. Not a coin." She thought for a minute. "I think I know who you could ask." She wrote down a name and address and handed the slip of paper to me.

I looked at the slip: Dwejra Ganado. #14, Triq Il Kosta. I'd have to let Vito worry about the address.

"Can I start working on your mast cap?" she asked.

I asked about cost, she said not to worry about it, it was mostly about soaking, gentle scrubbing, and patience. "After it's cleaned up, we'll see what we see." But then she sunk the hook. "Perhaps we'll ask you to loan it to the museum?"

"Perhaps," I said. I noticed she hadn't said anything about what the Egyptian one in the catalog was selling for. If the thing was worth a fortune I sure wasn't going to give it to a museum.

On the other hand, if it wasn't worth very much, maybe giving it to them was a fair trade for the information.

As I was leaving her office, I noticed a large photo on the wall of a striking, silver-haired woman with the legend: Dr. Dwejra Ganado, curator, 1975-2010.

***

"HI. OH! PERHAPS I'm at the wrong house." I looked back at Vito, but he just grinned at my discomfiture, as he seemed to do at everything. I looked down at the slip of paper: #14, Triq Il Kosta. But of course there was no number on the house.

We were at the old house south of the mosque that I'd seen from the boat. Up close it was indeed very old, but well maintained.

When I'd knocked, the door had been opened by a beautiful young woman, and I was stammering like a kid at the prom.

"Who are you looking for?" she asked, smiling.

"Uh, I'm looking for, um," I looked again at Elvis' note, and decided based on the caption of the picture to add the title. "Doctor Dwejra Ganado, sorry for butchering her name."

"It's easier to pronounce if you don't look at the spelling," she laughed. "You're at the right house, you're just about a year too late. My grandmother has passed away."

"Oh, I'm so sorry..." now what was I supposed to say? "I'm David Connor, this is Vito..." I realized I didn't know Vito's last name. I hurried on. "I was told that, er, Doctor Ganado, was an expert on antiquities, and I found something in the ocean, seems kind of old, and I was hoping..." I petered out. What was I hoping? I guess I was hoping her grandmother was going to tell me I had found Paul's lost ship.

She extended her hand, and something electric passed between us as we shook hands, or maybe that was just me.

"I'm Caroline. Why don't you come in," she said. "Bring your friend." Her voice sounded like she was always on the verge of laughing. Her English was excellent, but I couldn't place her accent. It sounded partly Maltese and partly American.

I gladly followed her shapely form and swinging blonde ponytail into a surprisingly cool parlor. The inside of the house was as well maintained as the outside, clean but not fanatically so, cluttered and well lived-in.

After seats and drinks had been offered and accepted and declined – Vito declined the seat but accepted the Coke and I did the opposite – she said, "Who told you to ask for Grandmother?"

25

"Elvis, I mean Elspeth, something, at the museum."

She smiled widely at the 'Elvis' gaff. "Elspeth Cachia. I think I'll start calling her Elvis, too. But did she really refer you to my grandmother?"

I showed her the slip of paper with Elvis' handwriting.

"Ah! I see the problem. You notice it does not say 'Doctor.'"

I was confused. "So, your grandmother wasn't Doctor Ganado?"

She laughed. "That's not what I mean at all! I mean Grandmother *was* Doctor Dwejra Ganado. Elvis is of my grandmother's generation, and she insists on calling me by my Maltese name. My grandmother was like that as well. Grandmother wanted me to be a copy of herself, I think. She's the one who insisted I be named Dwejra Caroline Ganado. She wanted me to be properly educated, which to her meant a degree in ancient Mediterranean history from a prestigious British university. So, naturally, I rebelled and went to America, instead."

That explained the accent. "So, I guess this is a wild goose chase," I said. Surprisingly, in Caroline's company it didn't feel like a waste of time at all.

"Well, not necessarily. I may not have my doctorate yet, but I didn't just surf in America. I studied ancient history at Stanford."

"Wow, Stanford! I mean, that's a long way from home. Great school, though, from what I've heard." Man, I sounded stupid.

"Yes, Stanford was fun, and of course San Francisco is lovely. But mainly, Stanford and Yale have the best ancient history courses in the world, and I thought the weather would be nicer in California than New England."

"So, Elvis did mean you, not your grandmother, when she directed me here?"

"Probably. I teach at Saint Paul's College. Ancient history, but I'm trying to get them to set up an archaeology department." She paused long enough to let that sink in. She was definitely the right person to talk to. "So, you said you found something in the ocean?"

I hesitated just briefly. I hadn't thought through the ramifications of this possibly being something a school might become officially interested in, but it was too late to back out now. I pulled out the metal bull piece and handed it to her. "What can you tell me about this?"

In an instant she was transformed from a folksy, hospitable surfer girl to a doctor – well, at least a master – of ancient history.

"Copper, obviously. Amazing it didn't corrode in the sea; it must have been alloyed with something. Some flecks of silver inlaid in the engraving. Perhaps it was all silver-plated initially, that would have slowed the corrosion. Too large to be a coin, and it looks like there may have been an eyelet at the top here." Anthony had pointed out the same thing. She turned it over and tried to read the writing on the back, shrugged and turned it back. "More likely an amulet or a medallion, what we would call a good luck charm. You know what this is, right?" She was pointing to the figure I'd taken for a bull.

"No idea." I didn't want to make myself look any dumber.

"Oh, okay. This looks like the Minotaur. And these circles around it represent the labyrinth." Blank look from me. She jumped up and rummaged through a pile of books and pulled one out. She flipped several pages then came over and stood behind my shoulder, leaned over and held a picture in front of my face. She smelled really great, and some of her hair tickled the side of my face. Pay attention, David!

Now that I knew what I was looking at, the picture was obviously an inscription of a man with a bull's head, inside a pair of circles. Even my untrained eye could see similarities between the inscription in her book and the engraving on the front of my medallion. She continued.

"Ancient Greek myths told of a Minotaur, a half man, half bull creature terrorizing the island of Crete. A labyrinth, a maze, was built to contain him. Dozens of representations of the Minotaur have been found, from coins to very large stone carvings. Most of them look similar to this, a bullheaded man with either two or three circles surrounding it." She turned the amulet over. "There's writing on it. The style of writing on the back looks like first century Greek, but I can't quite make it out. By the first century, of course, not even the Greeks were taking most of the myths seriously. They were more like – Paul Bunyan stories. So this medallion was probably something a visitor would buy as a souvenir of a visit to Crete. I wouldn't be surprised if the letters on the front turn out to be a name, and the

27

writing on the back might be a slogan like 'good luck' or 'good health to you.'"

I hadn't seen any writing on the front. "Is there any way to decipher the writing?" I asked. Finally, that wasn't too dumb of a question.

"Probably," Caroline said. "Come on." She led the way to a study at the front of the house. The view from her desk was directly out toward where I'd been diving the previous day. She placed the medallion on a flat black surface under a device that looked like an overhead projector.

"If you plan to have children in the future you may want to leave the room." My jaw must have dropped, because she quickly added, "Just kidding. No X-rays. Actually, it's something I cobbled together." She pressed a couple buttons on her computer, and a bright beam of red light blasted out of the part I'd taken for the head of the projector and lit up the medal. The light was slightly off center and rotated through 360 degrees, then changed to green and rotated again, then went off. She hit a couple keys on her keyboard, then flipped the medallion over and ran through the same process for the other side. Her computer screen began filling with dozens of images of the medallion.

"The red and green lights are lasers," she explained. "The camera captures all these pictures with the lasers at slightly different angles, then the computer begins overlapping the images until it comes up with a half dozen or so that have the best combination of contrast and resolution."

I just nodded. I knew a little about contrast and resolution from working with Photoshop, but she was way beyond me with this gizmo. The computer continued to manufacture images, and Caroline would occasionally click on one and drag it to the side. "Oh! Here we go," she said.

She clicked on one image and enlarged it to full screen. Using the mouse, she began erasing some of the details.

"These parts here," she said as she worked, "are just shadows created by the encrustation on the surface, so we can get rid of this, and this..." she worked on it for about five minutes. I heard Vito going into her fridge for another Coke. Finally, she said, "This is probably as much as we're going to see without taking more of the scale off. This line on the front looks like '*Las...*' If it's a place name, I may be able to find it. The letters I can make out on the back look like '*phyla...*' and there is more under all this encrustation. Several words that start with those letters mean something like 'guard' or 'keep.' If it's an amulet or good luck charm, it would make sense if it said something like, 'this will guard you.'"

"Is it just me or does it look like that '*phyla...*' is written differently, like a different font, from the '*Las...*'? I mean, if they had fonts back then."

She beamed at me like I was one of her students. "Very good, David! Yes, archaeologists do sometimes use the term 'font' to describe differences in writing styles on artifacts and potsherds, and these are definitely different. If I had to guess, I'd say the '*Las...*' on the front was part of the mold, and the '*phyla...*' on the back was incised by hand. But we'll know more after we get it cleaned up. Where did you find it?"

This time my hesitation was noticeable. What if this turned out to be significant? Could I trust her not to take over my dive site? She came to my rescue.

"That's okay, I don't need to know. Are you going to be around for a while?"

"Do you know Anthony's Dive shop?" She nodded. "I'll be in and out of there for the next few weeks."

"Do you trust me enough to leave it with me?" There was the twinkle in her eye again. Obviously I was being teased. But I didn't really know her that well, and I did have a question.

"Um, how much might this thing be worth? And what do I owe you?"

"Oh! I hadn't thought of that. Of course, you barely know me. Well, first, you don't owe me anything, as long as I can use the pictures in class if I need them. As to value, right now, Anthony or one of his friends would probably give your about twenty-five Euros for it."

"Oh."

"But you would not be wise to take it. First century coins sell for anywhere from five Euros to five thousand. But this is not a coin; I've seen thousands of coins, but I've never seen one of these. It may

29

be worth only a little, or it could be worth hundreds, or thousands, or more, depending on its significance and rarity. How about this..."

She printed a copy of the image we'd been looking at, then wrote across the face of it, "Received on loan from David Connor, one medallion as shown. To be returned within two weeks." She dated it and signed with a flourish, "Caroline Ganado" and drew a little smiley face.

"I'll bring it to you at the dive shop as soon I've cleaned it up."

I found I really didn't want to wait two weeks to see her again. "Great! But, Elvis said most of the cleaning process is just soaking and patience, so, er, what are you doing this evening?"

CHAPTER
4

THE DELAY AT SIDON put the small coaster even further behind the weather, and for the rest of the trip north to Myra they struggled to make headway. A passage that should have taken three or four days took almost two weeks. When they finally stepped ashore in Myra, Julius and his whole troop found it awkward walking on solid ground.

Myra was a grain port. Granaries there collected wheat from the countryside nearby as well as shiploads from Alexandria, Egypt, for export to Rome. Rome had a huge appetite for grain, and the government was the biggest customer. As a sort of welfare program, Rome handed out grain to poor citizens rather than monetary relief.

Fortunately, there was still one brave – or foolish – captain of a large wheat freighter from Alexandria preparing his ship to make a late season run to Rome. Every nook and cranny of the ship had been stacked with amphorae of wheat. Additionally, the crew had packed their cramped space, a cabin built above the bow, with water jars. More than enough for themselves; they hoped, if the voyage went on longer than expected, to sell water to passengers who hadn't brought enough.

In winter, the prevailing wind in the Mediterranean blew from slightly north of west toward the east. Sailing from east to west, then, required tacking: angling across the wind for a leg, then changing tack and angling the other way, gradually zigzagging upwind. Tacking, however, required that your ship have a firm "bite" on the water, a deep, sharp keel. First century ships, particularly broad cargo ships, tended to have rounded keels with very little sideways resistance. If a ship tried to steer too closely into the wind, the ship simply 'skated' sideways, downwind. Hence, it was impossible for them to maneuver directly upwind. If a ship needed to go west, and the wind was blowing from the west, the ship would just have to wait until the wind changed.

Wheat and other eastern Mediterranean goods got scarce in Rome in winter, and the prices went up. The captain of this grain ship, an Egyptian named Potut, was young to be a captain, but that was deceptive. His youth disguised a lifetime at sea and a keen mind. He expected to make his fortune with this late run. If all went well, he would be selling his wheat for twice what it would have brought just a month earlier.

In addition, Potut had already booked more than two hundred passengers. His ship had no passenger accommodations; they simply had to wedge themselves in wherever they could find a space. For years Potut had seen how much money flowed to ship owners waiting in comfort and safety back in Egypt while young men like himself risked life and limb at sea manning their ships. On those trips he'd learned how to make extra money, buying what was commonplace in one port and selling it in another where it was rare. Once he'd risen to the rank of captain, though entitled to the comfort of the cabin jutting up like an outhouse from the stern deck, he had instead chosen to rough it on the deck with the passengers and crew, and had packed his cabin space with clay jars of olive oil and wine from Judea. As his personal fortune grew he'd reinvested his money in ivory from Africa, purple fabric from Thyatira, and cinnamon from Lanka – sharing none of the proceeds, of course, with the ship owners. After several trips

32

spent in that manner, he had finally amassed enough to purchase his own ship.

It was an old freighter, well past its prime, but it was huge: one hundred cubits long, nearly twenty-five cubits wide in the middle, with a capacity of four hundred tunna. Driven usually by a foremast and mainmast, Potut could rig fore and aft staysails when the wind was right and gain an extra knot or two of speed.

Potut had spent little on upgrades, preferring to save his capital to invest in cargo. The only addition he'd made to the ship was a new bowsprit cap with a sculpture of Isis, the namesake goddess of the ship, cast into it. His hope was that, if the ship got into trouble because of his stinting on maintenance, Isis would take care of them.

Most ships of the day came to a point at the stern as they did at the bow, but Potut had chosen this old ship partly because it had a wide stern. The previous owner had decided to get rid of it after a particularly frightening episode in which a steep following sea had wrested control from him, and the waves had pushed that blunt stern blindly forward.

But Potut was fearless and to him, the broader stern meant only one thing: more cargo capacity. It also meant two steering oars, one on each side of the stern rather than a single one in the middle, which meant he needed two steersmen. He had investigated adding a tiller system, a complex of levers and pivots that would have linked the two steering oars and allowed one man to control them both, but the cost was prohibitive. Hiring an extra man cost far less, and the extra manpower was a fair trade-off for the fifteen thousand amphorae capacity of his ship.

He was in debt more than he was comfortable with, and now needed to make his ship profitable as quickly as possible. His cabin on this trip again held some expensive and rare items he knew would turn a profit in Rome – spices from India and silk from China. But that was more to keep up the appearance of normalcy for his crew. This trip he'd actually saved room to squeeze himself into his cabin. Instead of spending every spare denarius on trade goods, he'd gambled an unspeakably fearsome amount of money on one small special box, and he wanted to stay close to it.

It was roughly a handbreadth in width and height, about two handbreadths long, lined inside and out with lead and sealed shut. He had built it into the frame of his cot himself when the crew was on leave so that no one but he knew it was there. If his crew thought at all about why he was using his cabin for his personal space instead of for freight as had always been his habit, they probably assumed he was just getting soft. But the truth was that he wanted to stay close to his prize. On his last visit to Rome a dealer with connections to the palace had requested it, promising him a price that, combined with the wheat shipment, would net Potut enough for a brand new ship.

The ship was, in fact, grossly overloaded, but that was not unusual. Most captains would take all the cargo they could get. Sailing a half-empty ship was a losing proposition. If a ship was unsafe, people simply resigned themselves to it. The Fates either smiled upon you or they did not. His passengers weren't complaining.

***

JULIUS AGAIN SIGNED a chit for passage for himself, his guards and his prisoners, and Potut accepted it with a smile. He would be able to cash it while he was in Rome, rather than having to wait for payment. Luke and Aristarchus paid their fare with Jewish silver coins.

"I would offer to share my cabin, sir, but it is already nearly too crowded for me," Potut said to Julius. "I'm afraid you'll have to find space among the cargo like the rest of the passengers." By stressing *passengers* he was hoping the centurion would take the hint that he, Potut, was in charge, but Julius was having none of it.

"I'm sure whatever accommodation suits you will suit me, captain. I've spent more than my share of nights sleeping on the ground in battle." Then Julius added, "And on the decks of ships under my command. So, when will we be ready to leave?"

CHAPTER 5

IT WAS GETTING DARK as Vito and I set off from Caroline's on my rented Vespa. She had agreed to meet me at the dive shop at seven that evening to show me "the real Malta." I'm not an adventurous eater normally, but I would have gladly followed Caroline into an establishment touting chocolate-covered scorpions.

I was startled out of these happy thoughts by Vito pulling at my left sleeve.

"Mr. David! Look out!"

I had been too distracted by fanciful thoughts of Caroline, but now I noticed the scream of an engine racing close behind. I threw a glance over my left shoulder to find the grille of a car, headlights on bright, looming inches from the tail light of the scooter. Instinctively, I twisted the throttle to the stop, but a Vespa is not a Corvette, and we moved only a little faster. I felt the car's bumper impact the rear fender of the Vespa.

"Vito, are you okay?" I yelled.

"Okay, but hurry!"

Was this guy crazy, or drunk? I couldn't get my head around the idea of someone actually trying to kill us, but there was no time to think about it. The Vespa slowly accelerated, too slowly.

Ahead I saw a patch of road where the storms of the past two weeks had spread some sand from the beach over the pavement. I purposely stayed as far left as I could, hoping the crazy driver would

36

stay on that side as well. He did.

"Vito! Get ready to jump!"

At the last possible second I pulled the handlebars hard to the right and plowed into the patch of sand. As I had expected, the Vespa couldn't handle the swerve. I raised my right leg and Vito did the same as the Vespa tipped onto its side and slid through the sandy patch as the car flew past. We slowed considerably as we screeched toward the berm on the right side of the road.

The Vespa plowed to an abrupt stop. I managed to hang on to the handlebars, but Vito lost his grip on my shirt and went flying. I crawled off the Vespa and ran to Vito. He was fine, but he put a finger to his lips as he knelt behind a waist high clump of some of the prickly sea grass that formed a verge between the beach and the road. I crouched beside him and listened, but all I could hear was the surf behind us. Then, after about thirty seconds that seemed like thirty minutes, I heard the car engine rev and the car raced away to the north. Vito sat up and brushed sand out of his hair.

"I heard the car stop, I thought the man was coming back to check on us, but no one got out," he said as his breathing returned to normal. "That seemed funny, so I hid."

"You did great, I appreciate the help," I said. It couldn't really have been someone trying to kill us, could it? That only happened in movies. Probably some kids playing games, or a drunk driver whose conscience made him stop then drive off again when second thoughts about liability kicked in. He or she would probably be searching the paper tomorrow for news of two people injured in a Vespa accident.

The Vespa's handlebars were bent and it refused to start. By the time we pushed it back to town, it would be too late for my date with Caroline. Fortunately, my cell phone was undamaged, so I called her for a rain check.

"Oh! Are you okay? And Vito?" she asked.

"We're both fine, the Vespa's trashed. I'm afraid I'll have to cancel our date. Can we do it tomorrow evening?"

"I'm so sorry, I have an evening class tomorrow." Was she having second thoughts about dating the American tourist? "I'm free on Wednesday night, though."

"Great! I'll see you then." It felt like Wednesday wouldn't come quickly enough. Boy, David, you've got it bad.

**

AFTER A LATE DINNER for one I decided to check in on my Phoenix operation. Midnight was actually a good time to call Phoenix. Gary should still be at the office. Gary was my sister's perennially broke husband, and for three years he'd been my brother-in-law/ accountant/ office manager.

"Copper State Fire Protection, how can I help you?"

"Well, at least you haven't let the office burn down."

"Dave!" How's it goin' dude?" I hated being called dude even more than I hated being called Dave. "Hey, man, what time is it there? You must be out enjoying the night life, huh?"

"It's fine. How's the business?"

"Good, man, good. So don't hold back, tell me about sunny, uh, Italy."

"Malta. Saint Paul's Bay, Malta. It's fine. I left my itinerary on my desk, look it up on the interweb. How did you do with Sunset Palms apartments? Any problems?"

"Oh, you know, making progress. So come on, tell me about the chicks, the resort, the casino; I read the brochure. It looked awesome! Give me something!"

"You know I don't gamble. But yes it was awesome, and it was also expensive. I moved out of the hotel into a room in the back of the dive shop where I'm renting my equipment. It's a lot cheaper."

"What do you care about cheaper? Man, if I had your money I'd burn mine. You're on vacation, live a little!"

"I'm having a great vacation; I'm living a lot. In fact I moved to the dive shop to save money so I can stay here longer."

"Cool!"

"Yeah, cool. So. Sunset Palms." I knew he was hoping I wouldn't ask for more details. "You said you're 'making progress.' What does that mean? Exactly how many have you gotten done?"

"C'mon, man, lighten up. You're supposed to be on vacation."

"How many, Gary?"

"Well," he paused. "Eric quit, and Mark's been sick, so... we

38

haven't exactly gotten to it yet."

Long pause from me while I drew a breath and counted to ten. "Gary, there are four days left in the month. Sunset Palms has nine hundred extinguishers, and they all need to be certified before the end of the month."

"What am I supposed to do with just one guy? Vance is busy in Tucson."

"You're certified as an inspector; you and Chuck can do the whole complex in four days if you put your nose to the grindstone."

"I don't do that anymore, I'm the manager!" Well, he was the office manager anyway. About one person out of a thousand is allergic to the ammonium phosphate powder inside fire extinguishers. A year after Gary started working for me he got a face-full of it and discovered he was one of them. Or at least he claimed he was. He also had asthma, and I'd seen him go into a wheezing fit when there was even a little ammonium phosphate in the air, so maybe he was telling the truth.

"Well, you're also the accountant. What does your accounting tell you will become of the business if we start losing accounts the size of Sunset Palms?" I calmed down a bit. My sister would never forgive me if Gary quit the steadiest job he'd ever had. "Look, you know as well as I do that very few of the extinguishers at Sunset Palms will need to be refilled. Let Chuck do those, you can work on the rest without being exposed to any powder."

"Well..."

"Get it done, Gary. And apologize to Eric –" Gary started to object, but I knew Eric was a reliable worker and would only have quit if Gary ticked him off – "apologize to Eric and get him to come back to work."

He told me not to worry – unlikely – and then added one more tidbit.

"That guy Peter something, from Metropolitan, came by again. He said he's been authorized to raise the offer. I chased him off."

Metropolitan was our largest competitor and had made several attempts to buy me out. I had never been interested. With a lot of hard work and hustle my business had grown to the fifth largest in our crowded market. I liked the independence of working for myself. I know my employees were happier in the more relaxed atmosphere at my shop than they would be working for a big outfit like Metropolitan.

But my priorities seemed to be changing. Was it the treasure hunting, or was it Caroline? I'd only just met her, but I was feeling something I hadn't felt in a long time. Suddenly I wasn't as determined to keep my business out of Metropolitan's hands as I always had been. I was having a blast playing archaeologist. By comparison, checking fire extinguishers all day every day, while profitable, was mind-numbingly dull. Maybe it was time to do something different with my life. I'd had my nose buried in a job I didn't enjoy for years, just so I could make enough money to spend a few short weeks doing something I was passionate about. Was it possible my priorities were exactly backwards? Or maybe I was fantasizing about Caroline.

I told Gary, "Call Peter back and apologize to him, too."

"What?"

"Just tell him you are the wrong person to talk to, and tell him I'll call him when I get back from vacation. No, you know what? Give me his number, I'll call him tomorrow."

"Dude, you're selling the business? You can't do that!" Gary sounded positively panicked. No doubt he knew that new management would not be nearly as lenient as I was. He was probably right, but at the moment I didn't particularly care.

"It's my business, Gary, I can do anything I please. But I didn't say I was selling it, you did. Look, it doesn't cost anything to be nice. And it doesn't cost me anything to hear what the man has to say. Read me his card."

"But..."

"Just read me the card, Gary."

"All right, just a sec." I heard papers shuffling, then he read me the contact information from the Metropolitan business card. "So, what's her name?"

"What's whose name?"

"C'mon, man; the skirt who's got you wanting to sell the business."

"Gary, you've known me for five years." He had; I'd met him when I was taking scuba lessons. I'd introduced him to my sister before I realized how irresponsible he was and found a different dive buddy. "Have you ever known me to even have one serious girlfriend, let alone chase 'skirts,' as you put it?"

"No, dude. That's why I'm asking. You sound different."

"You don't know what you're talking about, and I need to get to sleep. Make the calls."

***

"SO, WHAT DID YOU think?" There was that twinkle again. A guy could get used to this. We turned left on the narrow sidewalk to stroll up the north side of the bay.

"That certainly was, oh, unexpected," I told her.

I had spent Tuesday and Wednesday diving with Vito, pulling up junk, beer cans, and the occasional coin. We knocked off early Wednesday so I could clean up for my date. Caroline had arrived at the shop on a Vespa of her own. I had offered to take her on the new Vespa I'd rented to wherever we were going. But she had parked her scooter beside mine and said it would be easier to walk. After my Monday mishap I couldn't disagree. She had led me from the dive shop west, around the head of the bay. I could see the Porto Del Sol restaurant up on our right. I didn't have the heart to tell her I'd already eaten there. I knew it would be full of tourists. But it had a good menu and a terrific view of the bay.

Then, just before we reached Porto Del Sol she took my hand and led me across the street to an establishment called Sammy's Tavern. I admit I held onto her hand longer than crossing the street required.

She was right, of course. Only a native would have known to look for such good food at a small tavern on the opposite side of the street from the tourists and the ocean views. Or maybe I loved it because I was enjoying her company so much.

"Hmm, so: unexpected. Do you mean unexpectedly good or unexpectedly bad?" she asked.

"Oh, it was great! You're right, I've walked past it half a dozen times since I've been here and never would have gone inside. But I can honestly say it was the best spaghetti with rabbit I've ever eaten."

"Perhaps because it was the only spaghetti with rabbit you've

41

ever eaten?"

"True; but still, it was the best!"

"It's a perfect metaphor for Malta. We were British for centuries, and they like rabbit, but Italy is so close by, so, spaghetti..." She turned her hands up and shrugged, actually looking somewhat Italian in the process.

"Why are so many of the names so hard to pronounce?" I asked as I glanced at a street sign: *Dawret In-Nawfragju.*"I don't speak Italian, but when I see it I can at least pronounce it, usually. But this is like – I don't know, Polish."

"Arabic, actually," she replied. I saw that switch flip in her again, as she went into professor mode. "We are not only British and Italian. Malta was dominated by Saracens – Muslims, from the ninth to the thirteenth centuries, so they influenced place names. After the Saracens came Italy, Sicily and France. Since none of those understood the Arabic letters they enforced the use of the Latin alphabet. After the English kicked out the French in Napoleon's day, most Maltese became conversant in English; but most also still speak Maltese. Which is how my grandmother and me, and many of us, became English speakers with Arabic names – Dwejra is Arabic." I caught the pronunciation that time: *'dwayra.'*

She again took my hand as we crossed the street, and then she abruptly pulled me back as a car screamed past inches in front of us. From my *right*. I had been looking the wrong way. That made me wonder if the near miss Monday afternoon had actually been my fault. Had I been driving on the right side of the road as I was accustomed to do in Phoenix? I couldn't recall. I told her about the close call Vito and I had had on the Vespa.

"Maltese drivers are famous, or infamous, for their crazy driving. You'll have to develop eyes in the back of your head," she said. "I wouldn't want anything to happen to you." I was very conscious of the fact that she was still holding my hand.

I didn't want the evening to end, but as we strolled along the promenade we eventually had followed the waterfront back to the dive shop. We turned, facing each other to say our goodbyes. Just as I was debating whether I should attempt to kiss her goodnight, she said, "Oh, David! The door!"

I turned around, and saw that the glass from the dive shop door was lying in a glittering pile on the ground.

CHAPTER

6

RIGHT FROM THE START, the wind fought them. Potut had intended to steer a course for the passage south of Rhodes and north of Crete, but with the wind out of the west he could only make any headway at all by staying close to the coast. What should have been a two-day trip at most – reaching from Myra to Knidus, the westernmost point on the southern coast of Asia Minor – took six days. Continuing west without the shelter of the Asian coast would be impossible.

"By your leave, Centurion," Potut addressed Julius respectfully, "I believe we are best served to sail south from here, into the lee of Crete. If the wind veers more northerly we'll be able to advance to the west. If the gods smile on us, the wind could even come around to the east of north." Potut had every intention of following that course, but it seemed politic to appear to defer to Julius. Rome was the customer for all this wheat, after all.

"I'm sure you know best what your ship is capable of," replied Julius. "However, let me confer with Paul."

"Paul." Potut frowned, trying to think who Paul could be. "You mean the prisoner, *that* Paul?" Potut couldn't imagine what advice a prisoner could possibly have on their course.

44

"He is much travelled, a wise man, possibly a seer," said Julius. "I value good counsel whatever its source."

Potut sent one of his men to fetch Paul. Julius had introduced Paul and Luke to Potut shortly after they'd gotten underway from Myra. Potut had noted the fact that Luke was a physician because that information could prove useful, but he had been too busy to give the balding, plainly dressed Paul more than a cursory glance. When the sailor returned with Paul, Potut took a closer look at him. He had to admit the man had an air of confidence. Not cocky pride or arrogance; he just exuded a feeling that there was nothing in the world he was at all concerned about.

"Julius tells me you may have some advice about our course?" Potut inquired. He did his best, but his irritation at having to listen to a prisoner showed on his face and in his tone.

"I'm no mariner, such as yourself, sir," said Paul. "However, I've sailed through the Great Sea many times before, and I've never known the wind to be favorable for making much westing this late in the year. Nothing about the current state of the wind gives us any reason to believe this year will somehow be different. We would be safest to winter here in Knidus."

Potut was determined to get his special cargo to Rome as soon as possible. If it hadn't taken that goldsmith so long he'd have sailed a month earlier. By now he'd be a wealthy man and wouldn't be in this worn-out freighter bowing to a centurion and listening to a prisoner!

But he didn't say any of that. He simply nodded, as though he were seriously considering the advice, and kept his own counsel.

"How about this," he suggested. "The wind will allow us to work southwest to Crete. If it stays against us we'll winter there. If the gods smile on us, we'll be better situated to continue our voyage."

"I assure you, sir," said Paul. "Your gods will have absolutely nothing to do with it. The God who created the world and all things in it, including the wind, does not act on whim or caprice. By His command the wind travels in reliable cycles.

45

Winter approaches; and no matter how impatient we are, in winter the wind always opposes westward travel. Pushing on endangers your ship and the people who have entrusted you with their lives."

Potut sneered, "Or, perhaps you are simply hoping to enjoy your freedom a little longer before hearing Nero's sentence on you?"

Paul said nothing, he just calmly looked at the captain for a moment, nodded to Julius, and then walked away.

"Enough," said Julius. "We will continue to Crete. Once there we will decide whether to continue to Rome or to winter in Crete."

CHAPTER 7

"WHO WOULD DO THIS?" Caroline was staring at the mess someone had made of Anthony's shop.

Maybe the same person who tried to run Vito and me off the road, I thought. She had nearly convinced me the near miss earlier in the evening, like the bump on Monday, had simply been a wild Maltese driver. After some time had passed, it had begun to seem unreal. But this break-in was a little too coincidental.

We stepped over the broken glass and through the now open front door of the dive shop. I couldn't tell what, if anything, was missing. I went to the phone and dialed 911. Judging by the sound it emitted all that accomplished was to annoy the phone.

"How do you dial 911 here?"

"112."

I started to dial 112, then stopped again. "Maybe I should let Anthony call the cops." I really didn't know him that well. What if he had secrets in the shop he didn't want the police to know about? "Any ideas how we can reach him?"

She reached for the phone book. "What's his last name?"

"I'm sure he told me, but, you know me and Maltese names. I think it was painted on the door, but..." I waved in the direction of the pile of glass.

She smiled and took the phone from me and dialed *41. A

conversation ensued in rapid-fire Maltese, then she hung up and told me, "He'll be here in a few minutes, he lives right nearby."

"How did you do that?"

She grinned. "American TV, detective shows. If he leaves the shop at the same time every night, I thought the last call just might have been from his wife; perhaps she called to tell him to bring something home for dinner, yes? I just dialed, what was it called in the states, Star six nine? Simple."

"Good job, Detective Columbo." I looked at the clock above the counter. It was a nearly midnight. "Bad news to wake up to, though."

While we waited, since I had no idea what might be missing from Anthony's inventory, I decided to check my own things in the back room.

"Well, the thief took my camera and my laptop," I told Caroline when I came back. "I can't imagine he'll get more than forty or fifty bucks for the camera, maybe a hundred for the laptop."

"No antiquities?" she asked.

David, I told myself, no matter how attractive you find this girl, remember your goal: finding proof of Paul's shipwreck. If you want to keep your dive spot to yourself, keep your mouth shut! Her first allegiance is going to be to her job and her country's history. Come to think of it, I hadn't even asked her what her take was on the biblical narrative. Perhaps she was one of those scholars who spend their lives trying to disprove the Bible.

"I didn't have anything of any real value. Oh!" I remembered the Saracen dagger. I looked in all the display cases but couldn't find it. I decided it was okay to tell Caroline about that since it had nothing to do with Paul; and I'd found it in Saint Paul's Bay, not the new spot. I didn't mention the mast cap. But of course there was nothing stopping Elvis from telling her about it. "I haven't found anything else of any real value except the medallion, and it's at your place. I haven't seen the Saracen dagger since I gave it to Anthony, so he may have it stashed somewhere else."

Anthony arrived in a rush, moaned at the damage and the mess, then noticed Caroline and seemed to draw himself up, as if he simply couldn't allow himself to be seen in distress by a stranger.

"Anthony, this is Caroline Ganado. She's helping me with the bull head medallion, and, er, we were just returning from dinner…"

"Delighted, my dear." He actually kissed her hand. I'd never seen anyone do that before except in movies. "Ganado… You must be the granddaughter of Dwejra. She was my very good friend." I couldn't help wondering, if ever Anthony met the thieves that trashed his shop, whether they would also turn out to be his 'very good friends.' Everyone else seemed to be.

"My condolences on your loss, my dear," continued Anthony. "Your grandmother will be greatly missed. I remember you now. But you were just a little girl the last time you were in my dive shop! I remember you being all arms and legs; the dive tanks were almost bigger than you were! When you put the mask on you looked like one of those guppies with the big eyes…" he cut himself off, perhaps fearing he was going to make her seem less attractive to me. I could have told him there was no danger of that. "Anyway, you are all grown up now. How have I not seen you?"

She laughed out loud. "I'm so glad you remember! I gave up diving when I discovered surfing. Then I was in America, and when I came back I was busy tending Grandmother, and since her death I've been teaching at the college…" I couldn't help thinking what an odd conversation this was to be having at the scene of a break-in.

"Anyway," he said. "To business. Wait here." He went into his office, then came back out a minute later. He said nothing, and from his face I couldn't tell if he was angry or relieved at what he'd found in there. Nevertheless, I was glad I hadn't called the police.

He then scanned his shelves and display cases. I asked about the *kilij*.

"It is safe. I showed it to some local people I know, but I'll probably have to put it on eBay to get the best price. Or I may just keep it."

I helped him lift up a tall, rotating rack that was blocking the middle of the floor. The masks, buckles, and small packages of replacement parts for regulators it normally held lay scattered on the floor. I started to pick them up but Anthony said to leave them. I broached the subject I had hesitated about earlier.

"Do you want to call the police?"

He appeared to contemplate that with a sigh. "No, I don't think

49

so, my friend. If I discover anything major is missing I might. But for now I'm sure they have bigger crimes to pursue. But you, you two young people have better things to do with your evening than cleaning up a mess that isn't your fault! I'll clean this up. You go out and enjoy the rest of your date."

"Well, it's midnight, the date's over, we were just going to bed. I mean, I was going to bed, Caroline was going..." Good job, David! Try getting your foot out of your mouth this time! "Why don't you leave the mess until morning, we'll all go to bed, and I'll help you clean up tomorrow?"

"No, my friend. This is my work, not yours. I never put off work. I'll clean it up tonight. Besides, you can't sleep here tonight with the front door wide open! I'm afraid you'll have to go back to the hotel."

Caroline interjected, "Don't waste your money on a hotel. I have a spare bedroom." Wow! Okay, she was definitely feeling what I was feeling. I don't know what showed on my face but whatever it was she added, "I promise not to attack you in the middle of the night."

That was not why I hesitated. In my head, I quickly ran through what I knew so far. First the hit and run, now this break-in at the dive shop. Was it really possible someone was out to get me? If it became known that I was staying with Caroline, would she become a target as well?

I hated to do it, but, "Thanks, that's a tempting offer, but I'll just sleep on the boat. Vito and I can get an early start tomorrow." Something unreadable flickered across her face, but she quickly covered it. Was she disappointed or relieved?

"That's probably better anyway, I have classes all day tomorrow. Come see me when you can. Thank you for a lovely evening." And she was gone.

So much for kissing her goodnight.

CHAPTER 8

THE WINDS CONTINUED TO mock all their attempts at progress toward Italy. The north wind at Knidus allowed them to lay in a course for Crete, but almost as soon as they reached the open sea the wind shifted into the northwest and threatened to blow them back to Palestine… or Egypt. Potut had to begin a tedious series of tacks just to hold the southwest course he needed to make a landfall at Crete. By the time they sailed into the sheltered waters on the southern coast of Crete his men were exhausted and most of the passengers were seasick.

Demetrius had been one of the first. He had sent for the physician the first day after they'd cleared the harbor of Knidus.

"I'm dying. Please help me," he claimed. Luke had examined him, prodding his abdomen, listening to his chest, measuring his pulse.

"Persons in good health should not take a physician away from those who are truly ailing," said Luke. "You're fine. If you are nauseous, it's only seasickness." He looked at the empty bowl beside Demetrius. "But if you were really seasick, you would not have so healthy an appetite." He turned to leave, and Demetrius grabbed his arm.

"Please, sir, there must be something you can do."

Luke rummaged through his bag and pulled out a piece of root. He cut a small portion off and handed it to Demetrius. "This is ginger. Put a few crumbs of this in your water, it will settle your stomach."

Demetrius thanked the physician profusely, bowing repeatedly, kissing his hand. He walked him to the ladder and held the doctor's bag for him as he climbed, then passed it up.

"You should also try to come up on deck," Luke added. "The fresh air would do you good."

"Thank you again. I'm sure I'll be fine now."

***

THEY DROPPED ANCHOR IN a harbor called Fair Havens. It was aptly named; the shelter it gave from the open sea was only fair. It was merely a half circle indentation in the rocky coastline, partially protected by some small islands offshore. If a blow came on from the south – unlikely at this time of year, but not impossible – the ship could easily be pushed onto the rocks.

"Haul in the skiff," Potut told his pilot and quartermaster Abu, a short, ugly man with broad shoulders and scarred fists who kept the crew in line. "Take a boat crew and check that the anchors are secure. Wood and water, and purchase some fresh food from that town over there." Potut dropped a small leather bag of coins into Abu's hand. "After we are restocked, you may give the men liberty. But set a boat crew to ferry to shore any passengers who wish to go. Just make sure you advise them that we may leave on short notice if the wind shifts. We will not wait."

"Yes, sir."

The small town proved to be called Lasea. It had grown up there because of some copper deposits, but most of the copper was gone now. The townsfolk eked out a living farming and fishing, and entertaining the few sailors who found themselves stuck in Fair Havens.

Paul expressed his wish to go ashore to preach to the people there.

"Cretans are always liars," said Julius. "Injurious wild beasts, unemployed gluttons. You'll be wasting your time. Didn't you tell me one of your master's sayings was something about throwing pearls to swine?"

"Jesus did say that, but he also said that you will be judged by the same measure with which you judge others. I'd like to meet these people and see for myself."

"I'd like to stretch my legs as well," piped up Demetrius.

"No," was all Julius said. No explanation was needed; Demetrius had by now proven to all the guards and many of his fellow passengers that he was nothing but trouble.

Julius summoned Otho. A chain was attached from Paul's wrist to Otho's belt, and they, as well as Luke and Aristarchus, were rowed ashore.

In town, Paul began speaking to a man in the town marketplace who was offering some woven goat-hair tent cloth. Paul invited the man to tell him about the ruins of the temple they had passed walking to town from the harbor, and the man told him about the gods worshipped locally, Asclepios and Apollo; he even spoke of the Minotaur as though it had been a god.

"Does it seem right to you that these gods, if they were really gods, would allow their temples to fall into ruin?" Paul asked. "Do you think the creator of all the earth dwells in a temple made by the hands of men?"

A lively conversation ensued that soon drew in several of the locals, until Aristarchus and Luke were also answering the questions of many of the people of the town.

Otho had heard this conversation between Julius and Paul over several days on board the ship. He unclipped the chain from his belt and dropped it to the ground, leaving Paul to his discussion, while he strolled from stall to stall to see what goods were being offered. A shiny trinket caught his eye.

"You like that, my large friend?" asked an ancient artisan. "Solid copper, real silver overlay, a good likeness of the

Minotaur, would you not agree?"

"I have no idea. I've never seen a Minotaur," replied Otho. He just liked that the large man – despite the bull's head – looked a bit like himself.

"Oh, there is no Minotaur anymore," the old man said. "But right near here, a thousand years ago, a great king called Minos prayed to Poseidon for a snow white bull, which he promised he would sacrifice to Poseidon. Poseidon granted his request, but Minos kept the bull for himself. To punish him, Poseidon caused Minos' wife to fall in love with the bull and mate with it, and her offspring was the Minotaur. The bull-headed man killed many people before he was trapped in the labyrinth." The old man pointed to the raised, silver circles surrounding the man-bull on the medallion. "See? The labyrinth. The Minotaur was finally slain by Theseus."

"Maybe you should be selling pictures of Theseus," rumbled Otho. "Anyway, I like this." He turned it over and saw more wording on the back. "What does this say?" Otho hated to ask, but he couldn't read.

"This says '*Lasea,*'" the old man said, pointing to the word above the Minotaur's head. Then he turned it over. "And this says '*Protector of the Minotaur.*'"

"But you said the Minotaur killed people. Why would you protect it?"

"Oh!" The old man winked. "I can see how you would take it that way, but it doesn't mean that. The labyrinth protected the Minotaur, but it really protected people from the Minotaur. You see? So I worded it this way so that if the Minotaur comes back, he will think that we are his protectors. What it really means is that Lasea," he waved around the poor, little town, "representing the labyrinth, protects people *from* the Minotaur, like this amulet can protect you from harm."

This was beyond Otho's grasp. "Could you make one with the same picture but different writing?' he asked.

"Certainly! I made this with these two hands, sir. I can make one any way you wish."

Otho told him what he wanted his medallion to say.

"But of course! Come back and see me at the time of the evening meal, it will be ready." As Otho nodded and started to turn away, the old man plucked his sleeve. "That will be one denarius, payment in advance for custom work, you understand."

***

"QUICKLY, THE BOAT WILL return at any moment!" Demetrius had used a probe he had stolen from Luke's bag to pick the locks on the manacles. He had been stealing clothing items from each of the guards over the past several days until he had assembled nearly a complete uniform, and he was now urging Aelius, the runaway praetorian, to change into it.

"We'll never get away with this."

"Yes we will. People see what they expect to see. You have the bearing of a guard. The boat crew will see a guard chained to a prisoner, not two prisoners. But hurry!"

The captain of the boat crew was not quite as thick as Demetrius could have wished. "I thought I knew all the guards. Do I know you?"

Aelius barely acknowledged the crewman. "Mind your place, citizen, and concentrate on doing your job."

Demetrius had been right; Aelius knew the perfect tone to take, a combination of superiority and boredom. He also, as Demetrius had advised, held up a couple sestertius coins, implying that the oarsmen would receive a significant tip for their services, and the boat captain acquiesced. "Oars out! Give way together." The crew began to pull for shore.

When they stepped ashore on the low stone quay that served the harbor, Aelius handed the boat captain the two sestertii, then turned and walked away, as if not caring whether his 'prisoner' Demetrius, would keep up. Demetrius stumbled into the boat captain, who held him upright and pushed him after Aelius.

The two prisoners made straight for the first building they saw, a barn, Demetrius pocketing the coins he'd lifted from the

55

boat captain. Once inside, Aelius began changing back into his own Praetorian uniform, but his efforts were hampered by the chain locked to his left wrist. Meanwhile, Demetrius worked Luke's probe into the lock holding the manacle to his right wrist. As soon as he was free, he headed for the door.

"Wait! You must unlock mine!"

Demetrius just grinned. "Sorry, mate. Thanks for your help." And he was gone.

Aelius found a hammer and chisel in the barn and began cutting through the chain. The farmer who owned the barn came to investigate the noise.

"What's this? What's going on here?"

Aelius drew himself up to the most dignified stature he could muster. "I am a guard from the ship in the harbor. My prisoner overpowered me, took my key and escaped. Help me out of this chain," he demanded.

"You seem to have one more set of clothes that you require. I'll trade you my help – and my silence – for the extra set."

After some haggling they agreed on the clothes in exchange for the farmer's help, his silence, and a day's ration of food. Aelius was on his way. His first order of business, he decided, would be to catch Demetrius and beat him to death.

CHAPTER
9

VITO AND HIS GRIN arrived at eight the following morning. I was barely functional after the late night and too little sleep.

We loaded fresh tanks and headed out to 'Blast a Giraffe.' I killed the engine about a hundred yards south of the rocks, and Vito dropped the anchor while I climbed into my gear. I must be getting old, I thought, this rig seems to weigh a ton. Vito Jumped in with his snorkel as I rolled over the gunwale and headed for the bottom.

Straight to the bottom. It struck me as I fell that I'd become complacent. Back in Arizona, on my rare dives I would check and recheck every piece of equipment before I went into the water. But now that I'd been diving daily for a couple weeks I guess I thought I knew everything.

My equipment check on deck had consisted of nothing more than hitting the power inflator switch. As soon as I heard the hiss and felt the buoyancy compensator begin to inflate against my chest I'd gone into the water. But ten feet down, the hose that ran from the BC to the inflator popped loose, and the all the air in the BC escaped out of the flapping end of the hose. I gave up on it and concentrated on swimming, trying to slow my descent. Another amateur mistake: I was clearly carrying too much weight. As the ocean floor rose up to meet me I managed to roll onto my back so that I hit tank first instead of face first. It helped a little, but I still hit the ocean floor harder than was comfortable.

I lay still for a minute, breathing deeply. Okay, still alive, my air was breathable and I had plenty of it. But I didn't want to even consider trying to finish my dive with a faulty piece of equipment. My dive computer showed me at eighty feet, deeper than I had been expecting to go. I rolled over and managed to stand up on the bottom. I tried swimming a few feet but I quickly saw I'd have to ditch my weights to get back to the boat.

My diving instructor had pounded one important lesson into me. The biggest threat to divers is not sharks. It's not running out of air. It's not even getting tangled up in something while underwater. The biggest killer of divers is panic. Before I pressed the button on the buckle that held one of my weights into its pocket in the BC I thought through what would happen when I did.

I knew I wanted to spend as little time at depth as possible, but at the same time it was critical to control my ascent. As I rose the air in my lungs would expand. If I dropped both weights I might rise too quickly and that expanding air could stretch, even rupture, my lungs. So, maybe a compromise; I'd drop one weight and see what that did to my buoyancy. Hopefully that would be enough to allow me to go up at a reasonable rate, controlling my position with my arms and legs. And if I was still too heavy I'd drop the other weight, which would mean working harder at control. As long as I remembered to keep exhaling as I went up I should be fine.

What I hadn't thought of was the possibility that the weight would refuse to release. The button, similar to the push button on a car seatbelt, went in and stayed in, and the buckle stayed latched. First the BC, now the weight buckle? What are the odds of two separate pieces of equipment failing on the same dive?

For just a moment, I panicked. I started jerking on the buckle on my right hip while mashing the quick release button. I switched to the one on my left hip and that button too went in and stayed in; the buckle didn't release. I began flailing and yanking on the buckles, my breath coming in large, artificial gasps.

Strangely enough, it was an additional scare that saved me

from myself. A shadow passed above me and I immediately thought, 'shark;' I knew sharks were a very slight threat to divers, but it would be better not to attract the attention of one by thrashing around. I stopped jerking at the buckles and just kept still and breathed. That cleared my head, and I calmly realized there was a simple solution to getting rid of the weights.

A dive rig dropped through my vision, followed by Vito's arm, then the rest of him. What I had taken for a shark was Vito coming to the rescue. Even with the regulator in his mouth he looked like he was grinning. He'd apparently seen me struggling, grabbed the other diving rig and jumped in without waiting to put it on. Like me, he'd been unable to stop his descent, but unlike me, this didn't seem to be troubling him at all.

I gave him the 'ok' sign, and pointed to my BC and drew a finger across my throat, to indicate it was kaput. Then I pointed to my weights and made the same sign.

He nodded, grabbed my vest with one hand and with the other pressed the power inflator button to valve air from his tank to his BC. Like mine, it began to fill then, as we watched, the zip-tie holding the hose to the inflator snapped, and the hose popped off. The BC went flat. Vito simply shrugged. Nothing bothered Vito. He looked a question at me. What do we do now?

James Bond may be able to get out of any situation with a knife but, since the advent of monofilament fishing line, most divers now carry rescue shears to get themselves untangled from lines and nets.

I pulled my shears from a pocket at my waist and began gnawing through the piece of webbing that the left weight buckle was attached to. Once it was cut I was able to slide the weight out of its pocket, but I kept it there for the moment and went to work on the right one.

Meanwhile, Vito tried releasing his weights and found the same thing: neither release button worked. He took his shears and copied what I was doing.

Unlike my rig, the one Vito had brought down had a one hundred foot coil of thin line in one of the pockets. I didn't have a lifting bag – an underwater 'balloon' divers use to raise heavy objects. I had pocketed the line instead in the optimistic hope that if I found something amazing that was too heavy to swim up with I could just tie the line to it, swim back to the dive boat with the line in hand, and then haul my treasure up to the boat.

I tied one end of the line to my weights. Vito wrinkled his brow at that, trying to figure out what I was doing, but he helped me make another knot in the line a couple feet away, to which we attached the weights from the second rig. Vito caught the loose fill hose from his BC and brought it to his mouth, pulled out his regulator and blew into the BC, then held his thumb over it while he drew in more air from his tank. I did the same with mine. After several breaths we started to rise. We dropped the four weights to the bottom but held onto the line. In this Rube Goldberg manner we worked our way up. When we got close enough to grab the anchor line we switched over to it and used it to control our trip back up to the boat, but I held on to the weight belt line.

Once on board, we hauled in the line with the weight belts attached. In the sunlight it was obvious why they had failed. Pulling the belt webbing away from the underside of the buckles, I could see that the projections on the bottoms of each release button had been cut off. The buckles could be snapped shut, but once closed there was no way to open them. The zip-ties that were supposed to hold the BC fill hoses onto the inflators were now lying on the bottom, but if I could have examined them I was sure I'd find they had been tampered with as well.

"Let's head back. I want your grandfather to see this." Vito nodded and hit the winch button to haul up the anchor.

***

ANTHONY WAS, OF COURSE, horrified to see the damage, but he didn't want to call it sabotage.

"Who would do such a thing? You could have been killed!"

"There's no way it was an accident." I replied. "I can tell you this: if I ever find out who did it, I'd like to take him diving."

But once again, Anthony seemed reluctant to call the police. "I'm just glad you're okay. I have brand new equipment on the shelves, take whatever you need. Take the best! I want you to be safe.

60

Both of you." He tousled Vito's hair, and began piling equipment onto the counter. Vito began tearing open packages, turning shiny things over, shaking, pushing buttons, installing batteries. When he'd satisfied his curiosity he started carrying the new goodies out to the boat.

Meanwhile I sat down with the instruction manuals of all the new items to make sure I'd know how to test each one before I went in the water, and how to use the stuff to get out of trouble if it arose again. What could have possessed someone to sabotage both dive rigs?

Whoever he was, he was no friend of Anthony's. He'd likely messed with both rigs simply because he hadn't known which one I'd be using.

Or, was it possible he was trying to kill Vito and simply hadn't cared about me?

**

I CALLED CAROLINE TO let her know my day had ended early. I was hoping I could take her out again and clear the air after the awkward leave-taking of the night before. But my call went straight to voicemail. I left a message but she didn't call back, and I spent the evening alone.

Vito and I were back at it the next morning with our brand new gear. In spite of all the poking, prodding and testing of the day before we nevertheless checked each piece thoroughly. Who knew whether the saboteur had been at it again?

That became our routine for the next few days: anchor, test, dive, then haul up the beer cans, coins, and unidentifiable pieces of junk, I mean rare historical artifacts, we'd found.

The coins ran the gamut from modern day change to silver coins from the past two centuries. A few were even old and intriguing enough to warrant Caroline's attention, if I could have gotten it. I missed her.

Did I really miss the girl, or did I miss the expert? Perhaps I was only wishing for someone to give me instant answers about the artifacts I found? As soon as I raised the question I had the answer. I could picture Caroline at home as I'd first seen her, in her comfortable old shirt and tight, worn jeans, barefoot, her hair swinging loose. I could still remember the scent when she'd leaned close, her surprisingly firm grip when she'd taken my hand as we'd strolled the streets of Saint Paul's Bay.

Definitely missed the girl.

There was another element to the daily dive routine. One morning, just before Vito and I took to the water I caught a glint reflecting off glass, coming from the minaret on the hill. Even though we'd moved further off shore the watcher was still there, apparently using binoculars or maybe a telescope. So every morning I gave the mosque a friendly wave just before I dropped over the side.

The next day's dive changed everything.

CHAPTER 10

INITIALLY, THE BOAT CREW tried to stick to their story that Aelius, the missing praetorian, had presented himself as one of Julius' guards tasked with escorting Demetrius to town. Abu 'reasoned' with them for a few moments, then came to Potut with what he'd learned.

"The prisoners bribed them, Captain," he said disgustedly. Two of the boat crew lay naked on the deck, their robes in rags beside them. Abu held his hand out palm up and displayed two shekels he found in the seams of their clothing. "The boat captain knew Aelius wasn't one of the guards. He claims Aelius gave him two Sestertii, but these were all he had on him, and he seemed to be genuinely puzzled where the other coins went. Shall I trice them all up for stripes?"

"You can deal with them later," Julius intervened before Potut could answer. "Gather a landing party and come with me," he told Abu. "I'll bring them back."

"You still have one prisoner on board that you haven't lost yet," said Potut condescendingly. "Maybe you should stay here and watch that you don't lose him and let me send Abu after your lost prisoners?"

"Paul will cause you no trouble. I'll take along one of them," Julius indicated the two sprawled oarsmen, one of whom was sitting up and trying to cover himself with the ragged remains of his tunic, "that one. Perhaps he can be persuaded to remember which way he saw Demetrius and Aelius heading." He turned to his guards. "Otho, come with me. Just in case some of these Cretans have notions of hiding them."

The only detail the bruised, half-naked oarsman was able to add to what he'd already told Abu was that, when he'd last seen them, it had looked like the two chained prisoners had been heading for a barn just visible behind the nearest house on the outskirts of Lasea. Inside the barn, they found a workbench and tools and, on the floor, the chain that had recently been attached between Demetrius and Aelius. Otho gathered up the chain. The barn's owner claimed no knowledge of the two but, at a nod from Julius, Otho calmly ripped the barn door from its hinges. Julius made it clear Otho could take down the rest of the barn in the same fashion, and the man suddenly remembered providing food to a traveler, and he pointed Julius toward the road leading inland from the village.

"Where are they getting the money?" wondered Julius.

"Demetrius is a pickpocket," replied Otho. Julius asked the barn owner to show him the coins he'd received from the two escaped prisoners but the farmer maintained he had only seen one traveler, and he'd helped him out of kindness, not for payment. Julius turned away disgusted, reconfirmed in his belief that all Cretans were liars.

Otho's next stop was the voluble merchant who had sold him the medallion with the Minotaur and labyrinth on it. The old man hadn't seen the escapees, but he advised him that one meal would not last the men far enough to reach the next town. Otho directed his men to go to each house and inquire about recent thefts, but after the owners of the first three houses all not only claimed to be missing valuables but asked for restitution, Otho changed tactics. He personally 'reasoned' with the three

64

householders about their supposedly missing valuables, and quickly got to the truth. After that example, the rest of the town folk made no claims of missing anything.

"They're still in town here somewhere," Otho reported to Julius. "They need more supplies for their escape."

In his time, Julius had developed a voice that could be heard by 500 men on a parade ground, and he used it now.

"Aelius! You have allowed this thief to mislead you! Turn out NOW! You are a Praetorian! You shame Nero and me by this conduct!"

Nothing happened for several moments. Then, the silence was broken by the creak of a gate three houses from the end of the street. Aelius walked out and stood at attention before Julius. "I apologize, sir. Demetrius persuaded me we were both fated to die if we continued on the ship."

"I'm aware of his ability to deceive. Fall in. Help us catch Demetrius and I may not mention this episode at your trial."

"The whole town knew instantly when you came ashore," Aelius said. "Demetrius separated from me as soon as we got here, but you may assume he knows, too."

Julius turned to Otho. "Burn that barn where we found the chain." Otho set off at once. Julius called the rest of his guard into parade formation in the town square, and they stood at attention until Otho returned.

As flames began shooting from the barn, and its owner began yelling for help, Julius called out again in his parade-ground voice.

"People of Lasea! You are harboring my prisoner Demetrius, a thief and murderer! If he is not returned to me before I count to ten, I will order my men to burn the rest of your town to the ground! One...two..."

There was a clamor and a flurry of movement from the last house adjacent to the road that ran north from the village, and Demetrius was thrown sprawling into the road. He sprang up and tried to rush back inside, but the door had been barred behind him. He took one look at the guards then started to sprint up the road out of town. Before he had travelled two stadia, the guards had caught him and knocked him down.

Otho unwrapped the chain from around his shoulders and handed it to Aelius. The man accepted it with as much dignity as he could muster and fastened the undamaged manacle on one end to his own wrist. He wrapped the damaged end of the chain around Demetrius' waist and held it while Otho stepped over and applied his massive strength. He twisted open a link in the chain, slid another link through it, then crushed the link closed again.

"That's too tight," whined Demetrius.

"Shut up."

Julius gave the order to march, and the landing party and guards headed back to the waiting skiff. "Hurry up," he said quietly, "the wind is changing, the captain will want to be off."

***

POTUT WAS INDEED anxious. He had already begun to weigh anchor. Paul approached him.

"Will you abandon the centurion?"

"The wind waits for no man," replied Potut, with less force than he would have wished. "Besides," he added sullenly, "I have a full cargo and over two hundred and fifty passengers, all anxious to move on." What was it about this unassuming little man that made him so nervous?

"You are the captain, of course," replied Paul. "No doubt you foresee much gain from completing your delivery." To Potut, it sounded as if Paul even knew about his special cargo, but that was impossible!

Paul continued. "However, the centurion paid for passage on your ship all the way to Rome. Are you willing to risk your own neck by angering him? What if news of your abandoning the centurion of the Augustan band were to reach Rome ahead of you? Of what benefit is it to a man if he gains the whole world but loses his soul? A man's life does not result from the things he possesses." Potut said nothing, but he held off giving the order to raise the mainsail.

When Julius was back aboard and the prisoners secured, he approached Potut and Abu to see what they intended.

"The signs are propitious," Abu was saying. He licked a finger and rubbed it behind his ear, in a superstitious belief that this act would prevent him thinking of a bad outcome. "I saw a white bird flying out to sea," he continued. "And I took the liberty of spreading some crumbs before the sacred chicken, which she readily ate. My conclusion is that this south breeze coming up is a gift from the gods. They are smiling on our voyage."

"It is not much of a gift," said Potut. "And it is from the south. Leaving harbor will require several tacks. If it strengthens we could still be blown against the cape there," he pointed west. "Still, I have no faith in the protection of Fair Havens for the entire winter. We may not get a better wind before spring."

Julius did not believe in superstitions, and he disliked the ogre Abu, but he wanted to be away. "I have every confidence in your skill, Captain. And in any case I doubt if we would be welcomed on our next visit to the town if we tried to winter here." He didn't deem it necessary to enlighten the captain on that score, and he couldn't be bothered to even acknowledge Abu.

Paul approached the trio. "Sirs, I perceive that navigation is going to be with damage and great loss, not only to the cargo and ship, but to ourselves," Paul said.

"We aren't going to try for Rome," Julius replied. "I agree it is unlikely the wind will stay favorable for that trip. But perhaps we can at least reach Phoenix." Phoenix was a larger town on the west coast of Crete. "There is a better harbor, and I can lock my prisoners in a proper jail for the winter." He had apparently forgotten that Paul was also a prisoner. Paul simply nodded and walked away.

It took all Potut's skill to tack out of Fair havens against the south wind. The old ship would only sail to within seven points of the wind so, after retrieving the anchors they sailed east south east, then wore ship to swing over to west southwest, each leg only gaining them a few stadia of sea room. Potut extended the fourth tack to the west southwest, and held his breath as they scraped past Cape Matala.

No sooner had they cleared the cape, however, than the wind died away completely and the sky took on a strange greenish hue. Some of the men began making signs intended to ward off evil. Demetrius began to whistle a tune, and a nearby sailor drove a fist into his mouth. "Never whistle on a ship!" the man said.

As if Demetrius' whistle had caught the attention of the gods, the wind began to rise again, but now from nearly the opposite direction: slightly west of due north. A cold rain began slashing down, increasing until Potut, standing near one of his steersmen, couldn't even see the figurehead that adorned the bow. The ship heeled hard over to port and began racing, out of control, to the south.

"Hold it steady!" he cried to the steersman, and threw his own weight on the oar, still hoping to aim the ship toward Phoenix on the west end of the island. But he had too much sail on, and the ship heeled dangerously.

"Hands to reduce sail!" he bellowed. Sailors ran to their assigned positions, Abu holding a short piece of rope, ready to 'encourage' any laggards. The yard braces were loosed, and the yard was dropped halfway down the mast.

There was no mechanism for reefing the sail; the excess sail bellied out into the wind, but its efficiency was somewhat reduced. To reduce it further, a sailor was hoisted up the back of the sail on a line draped over the yard. At roughly the middle of the sail he held the midpoint of a line while other crewmen drew the ends together in front of the sail to cinch in the excess sailcloth.

Still the wind rose. Finally, after resetting the sail twice more, Potut called for the exhausted seamen to drop the yard all the way to the deck and stow the sail. Since night had fallen, the sailors had to carry out this operation completely by feel. Toes and fingers got pinched and stepped on. Fingernails were torn off fighting with the rough cloth. Luke was called to deal with a sailor's broken arm. Finally, the sail was reduced to a neat, folded package that could be crammed below with the cargo. The rest of the crew fell exhausted to the deck and slept in the pouring rain.

***

WHEN THE SEA HAD KICKED UP and the ship began tossing like a wild horse the cook had thrown the burning embers of his cooking fire overboard. A sailor's greatest fear when out of sight of land was a fire on board a wooden ship. The crew and several of the passengers had slaughtered goats to offer to the gods, but with no way to burn their sacrifices they had simply dumped the carcasses overboard.

With the cooking fire extinguished, passengers and crew alike were obliged to staunch their hunger with whatever they had brought along that could be eaten raw. Some of the passengers surreptitiously broke open some of the amphorae and chewed on handfuls of uncooked wheat. Before long, most of them were 'feeding the fish' at the rail.

As night fell, Potut told Abu, "I want two topmen at the crosstrees all night. And I want their eyes fresh. Divide the night into eight watches and rotate the men regularly." Potut had yet to determine how fast they were moving, and he didn't want the ship to hit some unseen island while the crew slept.

"Yes, sir."

His crew including Abu was only 16 men, so all would spend some time aloft during the night. In addition, the steering oars required two men, who couldn't take the constant battering for very long either and so needed to be rotated out regularly. So no one on the crew was going to get a full night's sleep. Not that they would have slept much even if they'd had no work at all on the tossing, howling deck.

But better exhausted and alive than going to sleep with the thought of never waking up.

***

THE GALE CONTINUED without letup. Daylight brought no relief. Potut made his way from handhold to handhold over to Julius. "This wind is called Euroaquilo," he yelled over the wind. "When the wind blows from this quarter, with this much rain... I've heard stories of this wind lasting for days, even weeks. If you have gods, pray to them."

Julius didn't reply. He was gradually coming to Paul's point of view: there was only one God, and praying to other gods was pointless superstition. "God will save us, or he won't," he yelled back. "But I believe God has plans for Paul, so we will probably be all right."

As the wind continued to scream down on them from the north the sea grew more chaotic. But the experienced seamen among them felt a subtle change in the set of the waves.

"Land!" came a shout from the lookout at the top of the mast. Potut climbed to the crosstrees and looked where the topman pointed. After he spotted the land for himself he sent the sharp-eyed topman below for some well-deserved rest. Then he stared long and hard at the one solid feature in his wildly tossing world.

There was no sun to speak of, but it was about midday. He could now see that they were not in danger of striking the land; quite the contrary, in fact. To make a landfall there would require trying to alter the ship's course.

So, was it a landfall they wanted to make, or a lee shore they needed to avoid? Was there anything he could do to alter the ship's course in either case?

As they drew closer he recognized it. It was a small island called Cauda. It had no winter harbor; no harbor at all to speak of. But at least the wind and waves should lessen somewhat as the ship moved into the wind shadow south of the island. He made his decision, and dropped down to the deck.

"Haul the skiff aboard." Typically, skiffs were towed behind sailing ships if the weather allowed it, simply to leave more room on deck. It had the added benefit of preventing the boards of the skiff from drying and shrinking in the sun. But in the maneuver he was planning there was the very real possibility the skiff could be lifted by a wave and slammed into their side. Abu, with much cursing and flinging of his short rope, drove the crew to complete the task. After strenuous effort the skiff was drawn up to the starboard quarter where the crew hauled it on board. They then lashed it securely upside-down on top of some cotton bales piled on the deck.

"Hands to raise the foresail." A task that could have been completed, in good weather with a fresh crew, in a matter of moments, took them well past midday. When it was completed, the ship leaped dangerously ahead, but no one dared question the order. He then explained to Abu what he wanted to do, and Abu went from group to group of the passengers, warning them to make themselves as secure as they knew how.

Potut then doubled up the men on the steering oars and stationed Abu at the sheet restraining the tail of the distended foresail. As the ship's stern was lifted by the next wave he gave the command to the steersmen to push hard to starboard. The ship began to turn broadside to the waves. If it stayed there, the next big wave would roll it completely over.

The timing was critical. Potut needed to judge when he'd gotten all the leverage he could from the foresail. The ship needed to be moving fast enough that its momentum would carry it through the rest of the turn. Lose the foresail too soon and the ship would slow and be caught broadside by the next huge wave bearing down on them. Wait too long, and the wind would catch the reverse side of the sail and bury the bow of the ship deep in the water, perhaps never to rise again.

CHAPTER 11

"THE METAL DETECTOR WORKS really well. I found these in Anthony's shop," I showed Caroline some thin fluorescent yellow plastic spikes about two feet long. "I don't know what they are supposed to be for, but I've been using them to mark where I found stuff. Since I only have the one detector, I figured I can mark any place that sounds off, and you can dig. If we find a bunch of cool stuff in one place, it might be worth excavating deeper at that spot."

"Very scientific," she said, oozing sarcasm. She obviously had little respect for my archaeological style. "The proper way to do it would be to photograph the bottom, then set up a grid with spikes and string, then carefully sift the sand in each box of the grid."

"I don't have that kind of time!" Oops. "Sorry. I don't mean to be short with you." I stopped, drew a breath and started over. "I'm worried my brother-in-law is running my business into the ground while I'm gone. I'm going to have to get back to Phoenix soon."

Calls to the office in Phoenix had either gone unanswered or rolled over to the answering service. I could only hope it indicated that Gary was busy working outside of the office. But knowing Gary that seemed unlikely. And I was beginning to think that if I didn't go home soon my business might not be worth much to Metropolitan.

I thought I detected a look from Caroline that could mean she was hoping I would stick around, but that was probably my imagination. In any case it passed quickly, and her smile returned.

"Well, we'd better get started then, hadn't we?" she said. She peeled off her cover-up, revealing an athletic body in a European cut bikini. I jumped up to help her into her dive rig, then she went over the side.

***

WHEN I HAD FINALLY heard back from Caroline, the warmth of our first encounter was gone. I had invited her out. She had told me she was too busy and had invited me to her office on campus.

Seated before her desk like a kid in the principal's office I'd said, "I was hoping to take you out for a less dramatic evening than we had the last time." I'd said it with a smile. The smile wasn't returned.

"My schedule is pretty full. How goes your treasure hunt?"

Straight to the point. No niceties. The way she had said 'treasure hunt' told the story. She'd decided I was just using her. Clearly, if she had been developing feelings for me before, she'd gotten over it. Unfortunately, I couldn't say the same. I was – I think the old fashioned word was 'smitten.'

"It goes surprisingly well. In fact, I'd like to show you what I've found."

"What?" I had entered her office with my hands empty, so she had to be wondering how I was going to show her anything. I'd stood and pulled several old coins from my pocket and dropped them on her desk.

"David! You shouldn't be carrying these in your pocket, you could damage them!" I figured a couple thousand years at the bottom of the ocean had probably done more damage than my pocket, but I hadn't said anything. She picked up a gold coin. "Do you know what this is?" she had asked.

"Not a clue."

"This is an *aureus*. Gold. That's Tiberius," she pointed to what I would call the "heads" side of the coin. "It was minted from the years 14 to 37 and would have been in circulation for a hundred years or so thereafter." The enthusiasm had then dropped from her voice, as if

73

she'd suddenly remembered she didn't like me anymore. "A perfect one sold at auction a couple years ago for a hundred thousand dollars. In this condition, this one would probably bring between three thousand and five thousand."

What could I do to win her over? I wasn't ready to be kicked to the curb. "What about the others?" I asked. She hadn't looked at the other coins on her desk. I didn't really care, I just wanted to keep her talking.

"With the corrosion, it's hard to say." She'd picked one up and looked at it. "This one could be a denarius. It will need cleaning to be sure. I can refer you to a conservationist if you would like." She had just dropped it, and she ignored the other coins. "Was there anything else?"

Yes, there certainly was. I had sat back down.

"Caroline, I know you think I'm a treasure hunter. You probably think I'm just using your expertise to make a quick buck for myself." The look on her face said I had hit the mark: that was exactly what she thought. "But that's not why I'm here, I swear. I came here to see you."

"Well then, you've wasted your time."

"I'm not finished. I came here to see you in your official capacity. I think I may have found something significant, and I want to you to see it."

"These coins aren't proof of Paul's shipwreck."

"I'm not talking about the coins. It's something else. Something I couldn't bring to your office. You need to come out on the boat with me."

She hadn't said anything, so I had pressed on. "I also, I admit, came to see you for personal reasons. I truly enjoyed your company the other night, and I feel like an idiot for messing that up. With all that's happened to me since I got here, I lost sight of what I came to Malta for. I could have gone anywhere in the world for a vacation. I chose to vacation here because I wanted to look for evidence of the biblical account of Paul's shipwreck. I've been fascinated by it for years. I didn't come here to get rich. Frankly, I've lived a pretty simple life, and I have more than enough to continue doing so. All I'm trying to do here is prove that my dive site is historically significant. And

74

that's your area of expertise, not mine. I'd love it if we could work together on it."

She'd looked at me intently, no doubt trying to discern whether there was some ulterior motive in my request. I kept my thoughts and motives pure as the driven snow and hoped that was what showed on my face.

It must have, because she grinned, and said, "When do we go?"

Which was how we were now diving my spot together.

***

AFTER SHE WENT INTO the water I changed into my swimsuit and struggled into my dive harness. Vito, meanwhile, had jumped overboard with his mask and snorkel and was watching Caroline.

"Keep an eye on both of us, Vito," I said, and jumped. Not waiting for me to mark some spots for her, Caroline had begun exploring the sea floor around the markers I'd left on my previous visits.

On one of my trips back to the dive shop Anthony had shyly asked, "This Caroline, you like her, yes?" I agreed that she was a very fine person. "But, I mean, you like her? You could stay in her spare room? Or perhaps even her bed, yes? You don't need my back room anymore, do you?" Ah. That's what this was about.

"Anthony, we agreed, six weeks. And, not that it's any of your business," I smiled so as not to hurt his feelings, "but I am not sleeping with Caroline. I'm still using the back room, and when I'm not there I sleep on the boat."

"Ah! No, you misunderstand, my friend! I would not break our agreement. I was only asking because Father Jim has been asking where you are, when you might be leaving..."

"Well Father Jim will just have to make other arrangements for his hanky-panky."

"Hanky-panky? I don't know this word."

"It means... what 'Father' Jim does in your back room."

I told Caroline about it when we were eating our lunch on the boat. She didn't need an explanation of what hanky-panky was. "It's a

75

small place, Saint Paul's Bay," she said. "I'm sure Father Jim thinks his business is secret, but most everyone knows about his trips to Anthony's back room. There is a lot of speculation about who his partners are but he's careful with that secret. Probably he picks up tourists from time to time."

***

DURING THE DAYS I HAD been diving with only Vito for company I'd found more than just the coins I'd shown Caroline. I found a length of chain about six feet long with what looked like a complete locking mechanism at one end. I'd taken several pictures of it but left it on the bottom. I'd spent several evenings comparing my photos to images on the internet and was convinced it was Roman, a slave or prisoner manacle. I wanted Caroline to find it. And I'd told her the truth about finding something else that I couldn't bring to her office. We'd anchored nearly on top of it. It shouldn't take her too long to discover it for herself.

Before I could steer Caroline toward the chain she suddenly started excitedly waving to catch my eye. I swam over to her and she pointed at the bottom. I offered the metal detector but she waved it away. She pointed to her eyes, then to the bottom, then made an undulating gesture with her hand, like she was petting a dog. She had definitely found what I wanted her to see. The mud on the bottom, instead of being flat as it had been so far, was wavy. There was a field of regular humps about a foot high, a couple feet long, one after the other. I knew it must have some significance, but it needed the trained eye of an archaeologist. It was enough to spark Caroline's interest. We swam closer to it.

The wavy patch formed a rough rectangle about forty feet wide and about twice that long. One of the short sides of the rectangle was only twenty yards or so from the shoal water behind the 'blast a giraffe' rocks, and the rest of the field angled out to sea from there. Caroline was digging in the mud at something near one of the humps. When the water cleared she took a couple pictures, then lifted a chunk of something brown that I couldn't identify. I could see that one edge of it was a portion of a perfect circle. Had to be man-made. She

76

pointed to my camera and held up the curved brown piece while I shot it. She gave me a thumbs-up and dropped the thing in her dive bag and took the camera from me. She took several photos of the weird humped formations then headed for the boat.

I knew she couldn't wait to look at her find in sunlight, but I had other plans for her. I caught her arm and pointed to my metal detector, then back toward the chain. She photographed the chain, then picked it up. I waved the detector over the bottom where the chain had been, and it beeped again.

Caroline started digging, but I stopped her. I pointed to the air gauge on her wrist. We were both getting low on air. We dropped the chain back where it had been to mark the spot and headed to the surface. Vito saw us coming and helped Caroline board. He didn't care that his ten Euros a day was coming from me. He was Caroline's slave. By the time I got aboard and shucked my harness, Vito had dumped my dive bag on the deck and was sorting through it. He seemed disappointed at the shortage of beer cans and was sorting through the other junk, no doubt hoping to find something to show Caroline.

Caroline was practically bouncing up and down. "Do you know what this is?" I was really starting to love that bubbly enthusiasm. I had hoped for that kind of enthusiasm for the Roman chain, but she appeared to have forgotten all about it. Instead, she was holding up the curved piece she had found.

"Do I get to touch it, or do I have to guess from over here?" I reached for the piece, but she laughed and held it beyond my reach.

"This, David, is an amphora! Not the whole thing, obviously, but this is the mouth of the jug," she pointed to the smaller, broken curve. "And this," she pointed to a loop appended to one side, "is the handle. And it's stamped!"

"Stamped?"

"There were probably millions of amphorae made over the centuries, and hundreds of them are in museums. Mostly we have to classify and date them by the details: the size and shape of the handles, the mouth, the rim, the shoulder. Scientists have even catalogued the microscopic composition of the clay, so in some cases you can get origin information that way. But sometimes, the handles are embossed with the place of origin. I'll have to look this one up when I get home, but I've been staring at pictures of first century artifacts from Myra, Crete and Egypt every night since we met, and I'd be willing to bet this stamp is from Myra!"

"Which means what?" I asked. I liked the idea she'd been thinking about me ever since we met.

"By itself, nothing. But did you see that debris field down there?"

"You're talking about those weird humps on the sea floor?"

"Right. I could be wrong, but I think we're going to find that those 'weird humps' are dozens, if not hundreds, of whole amphorae."

I decided the chain, and whatever lay under it, would have to wait.

***

WE STOPPED ABOUT sunset. Caroline promised dinner at her home. Vito raised the anchor and we motored over to the beach, where he jumped over the bow and planted the anchor firmly behind a clump of sea grass. Caroline pulled on her cover-up and followed him. I made sure the boat was buttoned up and jumped after them. I missed the beach and landed in the water, but I was getting better at planning for contingencies. I'd kept my shoes in one hand and a towel in the other. I dried my feet and put my shoes on.

As the three of us were crossing the road to head to Caroline's house for research and supper, a man wearing a white robe and skullcap came out of the mosque and began screaming at me in Maltese. Caroline answered him calmly, but he ignored her and continued directing his diatribe at me.

"He says you are stealing holy relics," Caroline translated.

"Stop," I told her. "I haven't met anyone on this island yet who doesn't speak English. If what he's trying to communicate to me is so important, he can say it in a language I understand."

"You great Satan! I watch you and whore steal Saracen old things from our mosque!"

"Whoa!" I stepped forward so that I was between him and Caroline. "Call me great Satan if you want, but you have no reason to insult my, er, girlfriend." Whoops. "Just calm down. Now, what makes you think I'm stealing anything from your mosque?"

"I watch! You diving on mosque beach, bring up old things, things from Saracen battle long time ago. These things belong to mosque!"

I spread my towel on the ground and started pulling stuff from the dive bag: Beer cans, a dozen old coins and the same number of more recent coins, and an encrusted, unidentified metal thingamabob. Caroline had held onto her amphora handle.

"First," I said, "it isn't your beach. It's a public beach." I wasn't actually sure about that, but it seemed reasonable to me. I continued, "It's the Mediterranean. You don't own it," I said, as calmly as I could. "Secondly, do you see anything here that looks like it dates from the Siege of Malta? If you do, you can have it." The man scowled and examined the stuff on the towel but said nothing. "And third," I pointed to the trash. "If you guys own this beach, you're going to have to explain the beer cans to me. I thought you didn't believe in drinking." Caroline shot me a warning glance at that last remark, and she was right, my sarcasm was going to get me in trouble one day.

"Anthony showed me *kilij*. He said you find! You searching for Muslim old things!" Ah, the light began to dawn.

"Yes, I found a *kilij*; not here, I found it in Saint Paul's bay." I pointed vaguely north, and continued. "I am not, NOT, looking for 'Muslim old things.' I'm looking for things much older, *Christian* old things. Look," I said. I reached over and took the amphora from Caroline. "This is first century. First century, you understand? Five hundred years before the prophet. Fourteen hundred years before the siege. *This* is what I'm looking for. And I'm going to keep looking, on this beach. This is NOT your private beach." I put my artifacts back in the bag and rolled the towel back up. I took Caroline's arm and walked around the irate Muslim. Vito had disappeared quietly at some point during the fracas.

"We don't know that this is first century," she said quietly.

"I know, I was just trying to make him understand."

"Well," she said, "you may have temporarily confused him, but I don't think we've seen the last of him. In fact," she paused.

"What?"

"Well, you're right, the beach doesn't belong to the mosque.

But..."

"Wouldn't the mosque's property line stop at the road? Or at least at the water's edge? I don't see how he can claim to own stuff we've found several hundred yards offshore."

"You're right, he can't. But that's not the problem."

"So, what is the problem?"

"I got so caught up in all this... We'll talk about it after we eat." Now she had me worried.

CHAPTER 12

WHEN HE JUDGED THE TIME to be right, Potut signaled Abu. There was no time for a crew to lower the foresail. Instead, Abu whipped his razor-sharp knife across the sheet holding the bottom of the foresail, and the sail blew out like a flag, attached only to the yard at the top. In moments it had beaten itself to tatters in the shrieking wind.

The bow continued its turn, and it did bury itself in the next wave – but not too deeply – and a wall of green water poured down the length of the deck. Abu disappeared from sight, but, as the water drained off the deck and ran out of the scuppers, Abu's hard brown hand appeared clutching the belayed end of the sheet he'd just cut. A goat and a few chickens, as well as much of the cargo that had been on deck, were swept over the side by the wall of water.

The wave continued to roll aft. A woman screamed as her baby was torn from her grasp and swept over the rail. With no hesitation, Otho sprang up, grabbed hold of a line and dove overboard. He hadn't checked whether the other end of the line was attached to anything. He had simply reacted. He had learned to swim as a child in the Tiber in Rome and, like every other physical task, he'd excelled at it. The ferocious waves gave him no pause whatsoever.

The watchers on deck anxiously held their collective breath waiting for Otho to surface. Several of the sailors leapt to the line, one end of which was, in fact, belayed to a thole pin below the rail. They hauled on the line together, and Otho's head appeared above the water. There was no sign of the baby. As the ship tossed one way and the waves another the sailors gradually hauled Otho back to the ship. When he was within reach, he pulled himself up the rope with one hand, while the other protected the front of his tunic. The young mother came running up as Otho alighted on deck. He opened the top of his tunic and removed the child, who was clinging to the copper medallion hanging around his neck.

***

THEY WERE STILL BEING pushed to the south, though at a slower rate now that they had their bow facing into the wind and waves. In the back of Potut's mind was the concern that they could be blown all the way to the north coast of Africa. But Potut had a new, more immediate concern.

A wooden ship at sea is not quiet, but its various creaks and groans are familiar. Now, however, Potut was hearing new sounds. As he stood near the starboard steering oar and looked forward over the length of the deck, he could see a looseness, a twisting, of the wooden deck. He signaled to Abu, who clawed his way handhold over handhold to the captain.

His hands occupied, Potut jutted his chin at the deck amidships. Abu looked where he pointed. "She's working."

"She is," Potut acknowledged. "Too much. I'm afraid we must undergird the ship if we are going to survive."

He knew what he was asking. It would be a near-impossible task with the ship dancing as it was. On the other hand, why would anyone have practiced such a maneuver in calm seas?

Abu acknowledged the order without argument and went to make the needed preparations. He set two men to chopping away a small space in both rails amidships. Meanwhile, he got the rest of the crew to drag up great masses of rope. One long line was faked into two coils, one on each side of the bow.

Abu tied a small weight to the center of the line, then secured the line to his girdle with a piece of twine and began crawling out onto the bowsprit, which whipped like the tail of an angry cat. When the bowsprit rose to the top of its arc, Abu was nearly sixty cubits above the waves; when it reached the bottom of its path he spent what seemed like an eternity holding his breath as the bow was buried by the next wave. It took three such cycles before he reached the extreme end of the bowsprit. He patted Isis' face on the bowsprit cap and locked his legs into the stays. Then he untied the twine and drew the line up from his waist and held it above his head. When the bowsprit rose toward the sky again, Abu heaved the line out over the end of the bowsprit so that it fell into the water across the path of the ship. He had taken the precaution of tying a small weight to the line so that it sank quickly beneath the ship, and the coils of line on each side of the bow began paying out. As he scrambled off the bowsprit, the men he had stationed beside the two coils walked the line back to the middle of the ship. Their task was to keep the line dangling loose enough to avoid getting hung up on barnacles and other obstructions on the keel.

The sailors who had chopped away the rails had also padded the scuppers – the edges where the deck met the ship's sides – with bolsters of sailcloth. When the two crews holding the line reached the gap in the rail, they quickly drew in the two ends of the line over the bolsters. Both ends were reeved through the capstan and every available man fell to the capstan bars. When the line encircling the hull drew as tight as a harp string the two ends were secured to each other.

Potut could see that the deck was working less, but it was still working, twisting and flexing far more than the ship's builders had ever intended. He shook his head and ordered Abu to take two more fraps around the ship's hull. It took the rest of the daylight, but in the end he was satisfied they had done all they could to keep the hull from breaking apart during the night.

Now he could focus on stopping, or at least slowing, their drift toward Africa. He waved Abu over again.

"We're still being pushed south. If this storm continues much longer we'll, end up on the sands of Syrtis."

Abu agreed. "Sea anchor?"

"Get it done."

Abu knuckled his forehead and went off to set a crew to rigging the sea anchor. They attached ropes to the corners of a twenty-five cubit square of sailcloth, then brought the four lines together so that the sailcloth formed a bucket about three times the height of a man. Abu lashed a six cubit spar across two diagonal corners of the 'bucket' to ensure it remained open. The lines were attached to a rode made from their longest anchor cable, then the sailcloth bucket was dropped over the bow. They allowed the anchor cable to pay out about four times the length of the ship, then snubbed it down. The drag the sea anchor provided slowed the ship's southward movement and the stretch of the cable evened out the up-and-down motion of the bow.

Still Potut wasn't satisfied. The enormous waves continued pounding down on them from the north. He ordered the ship's carpenter to sound the well. Nearly two cubits of water was slopping around in the hold. His new ship – if he survived this voyage – would have one of the new Roman chain pumps, but this ship had none. His crew was exhausted. He set the prisoners and guards to work hauling up and tossing to leeward bucket after bucket of water. He was surprised to see Luke, Aristarchus, and even Julius join Paul and the rest in bailing.

If they survived the night, if the storm still raged tomorrow, he would have to think of something else.

CHAPTER
13

"DAVID." SHE SAT DOWN beside me on the couch with a cup of coffee in her hand. "I know you are not going to want to hear this."

We had prepared a terrific meal of *aljotta*, a fish soup, and *bragolli*, thin strips of beef stuffed with ground beef, hardboiled eggs, and bacon, working companionably in her kitchen like – well, not exactly like a well-oiled machine. More like a good cook and her inept helper. After dinner she served pieces of something similar to cheesecake. I had retired, stuffed, to the couch.

"You said in my office you wanted to work on the site together. When you brought me the medallion, it was interesting, a mystery to solve. Possibly worth some money to repay you for your investment in your equipment, your vacation, and so on. And I was happy to see you reap a reward for your hard work. And I thought that all you were likely to find was more trinkets like that. But now..."

"Is it readable yet, by the way?" I interrupted her. I knew where she was going with this. She was still thinking of me as a treasure hunter.

"Not yet, but it's coming along." She jumped up and went to retrieve it from her study. It seemed she wasn't ready to get to the point yet, either. I would let her deal with this at her own pace.

She came back, wiping the medallion dry on a hand towel, and sat down beside me on the couch. She leaned her weight on one hand on my thigh while her other hand held the medallion in front of us.

"The upper word on the front is now '*Lasa*...' If it's a place name, I haven't found it yet, but I'm still looking. Then on the back is another word we didn't see at all the other day, '*oth*...' something. That could be *othonia,* 'linen cloth,' but there isn't really room for that many letters under this encrustation, and I can't imagine what linen has to do with the Minotaur. A better guess would be *hothen*, 'from.' If it turns out to be that, then the *Lasa*... word could be a person's name, and the *phylak*... on the next line could be a place name. 'So-and-so from such-and-such a place.' But I'm pretty sure *phylak*... is going to turn out to be *phylake*, guard or protector."

Something niggled at my memory. "Do you have a Bible?" I asked. She headed back to her study, and I followed her. She dropped the medallion back into the basin it had been soaking in, then pulled an English Bible from the shelf and handed it to me. I turned to Acts chapter twenty-seven and scanned quickly down through the verses.

"Yes!"

"What?"

"Look!" she moved in next to me and looked where I was pointing, and I read verse eight out loud: "'We came to a certain place called Fair Havens, near which was the city of Lasea.' In Greek, that would be *Lasaia*, right? And you said the Minotaur was a Cretan myth. If that word on the medallion turns out to be *Lasaia*, that would make it almost certain this is from Paul's shipwreck!"

She smiled, but her reaction was much more subdued than mine. "Let's go back to our coffee."

When we were again situated on the couch, she took my hand and said, "David, as I started to say before, I'm happy for you, finding your treasures with your metal detector. I got caught up in your enthusiasm, and I guess I wanted to be a treasure hunter too. Also," she reddened a bit at this, which made her all the more attractive. "I am enjoying your company, and I don't want you to leave.

"But you have to understand, I represent the college. So far, you have found the possibly Egyptian bronze piece you told me about that you left with Elvis, the medallion, possibly from Crete, and we have the Amphora handle definitely from Myra, all found in the same place. Today you told that awful Muslim man that no one owns the ocean. But in fact, until you are twelve miles off shore, you are diving

86

in *Maltese* waters. I am Maltese; I have an obligation to my country. What if this is an important archaeological site? You can't simply say, 'finders keepers.' I must report it to the college. You understand, right?"

I was puzzled. I had hoped she now understood my change of heart, from treasure hunter to serious researcher. But apparently she still believed I was only here for the reward and needed convincing.

"As I said in your office, I really just came here to find some proof of the biblical account. I know I got caught up in the thrill of the hunt. For a few days there I was thinking I was Indiana Jones, but I'm over that."

"You would look good in the hat," she said. "But Indiana Jones was a fictional character. Not dearly loved by real archaeologists, by the way. In those movies he was actually something of a grave robber. Imagine, if the Nazis hadn't interfered, what was he planning to do with the artifacts he dug up? Take them, steal them, really, from Egypt and deliver them to his university. A gain for Princeton but a loss for the people of the countries he took them from."

"I get that. I'm with you, all the way. But," How could I make her understand? "I was hoping this would be a project that you and I could work on together. We are so close to finding something really cool! I don't want to just hand it over to a bunch of academics. Present company excluded, of course."

"Of course. I'm not trying to steal credit for your site from you. If you were staying here, on Malta, I'd love for us to work together. I don't want to drive you away." As if to reinforce that idea, she leaned closer and kissed me. "Please stay." I wasn't sure if she meant please stay on Malta, or please stay the night. And I wasn't sure I wanted to clarify the point.

"How about this," she said. "We dive the site one more day, just you and me, and I'll turn a blind eye to whatever your detector finds. If anyone from the school asks, I can tell them you mostly find beer cans, right?"

"Right."

"But I want something in return." She gave me that devilish look. "In exchange, you help me to try to bring up an intact amphora. Then I can take the amphora to the director –" she meant, I suppose, the director of the History department at her school, " —and see if he wants to fund a dig. If the school is not interested, then there should be no objection to your continuing on your own."

"Sounds like a plan." It did, but it sounded like a plan that involved either Caroline getting her wish for an archaeology department, and her college running the operation after I'd gone back to Phoenix; or Caroline going back to her office while I, with Vito watching my back, played around with my metal detector like a tourist until the end of my vacation. A week ago, that would have been fine. Now, carrying on without Caroline didn't have much appeal.

I had succeeded in my business despite my lack of a college degree. I could hold my own in a conversation with most college grads. But there were times when I was acutely aware of the gulf between myself and those with letters after their names, and this was one of those times.

I stood up to go. Metropolitan was expecting my call, expecting me to finally be willing to sell them my business. Had I really been thinking of selling my business? What was I supposed to do with myself – move to Malta and become a metal-detecting beach bum?

"Well," I said. "It's getting late, I should get back to the boat."

"David, the boat is secure. The sea was calm when we left it, and there is no weather expected tonight." I started to object but she cut me off. "And, no one is going to steal it. Everyone knows it's Anthony's boat. Besides, it's an island. Where would a thief take it?" she saw me hesitating. "I'm afraid if you go now, you'll decide overnight that this is just a vacation fling, and it would be best not to see each other anymore." That was exactly what I'd been thinking. "That is not how I feel. I don't want lose you. Please stay." She came to me and wrapped her arms around my neck, as if to prevent me from leaving.

I felt the tension in my shoulders subside. I was being a jerk. "I'm not going to spend the night. I don't want to give any more fuel to Anthony's overactive imagination. But I promise, I'm not going to go away mad."

"You're sure?"

"Is there any more of that cheesecake left?" I asked.

She grinned. I was really falling for that grin. "It's called *Pastizzi*

Rkotta. I'll get some. How about some brandy to go with it?"

***

BY THE TIME I GOT to the boat it was after 1:00 a.m. The boat, as Caroline had said it would be, was fine. The small waves had rocked it free where I'd beached it, but the anchor jammed into the clump of sea grass held it firm. I grabbed the painter and drew the boat close enough to get on board without getting wet. I made up a bed of floatation cushions across the stern, shed my clothes and crawled into my sleeping bag.

I was just drifting off when a small sound woke me. What was that, I wondered. Sounded like a car, but cars went by on the road every few minutes and I had tuned them out.

This noise was a car coming to a stop. I decided I'd better investigate. I climbed out of the sleeping bag. I was reaching for my shirt when I saw, arcing through the air, a bright spot of flame, heading right for the boat.

It hit the bow, shattered, and the boat became an inferno.

CHAPTER
14

POTUT HAD FALLEN INTO HIS bunk about midway through the last watch and slept like the dead, pausing just long enough to check on his secret stash. He had managed to drown out the wind, the waves, the creaking of the old ship, and the myriad other noises being generated by the storm. But he came instantly awake when the watch changed.

The ship had survived the night, but she was wallowing like a pregnant cow. He called the carpenter, who informed him that even with the prisoners and guards bailing with everything that would hold water, the bilge still had nearly three cubits of water in it. No major leaks, just a thousand small ones from the working of the old timbers.

Potut acknowledged the report. "Put all the passengers to it. If any object, advise them they are free to step over the rail and look for other transport to Rome. Make a hundred more buckets. It's all that is keeping us afloat. Besides, the work will keep them warm."

He stood looking at the cluttered mess the storm had made of his deck. He'd probably lost a third of his deck cargo. The big guard, Otho, had made a nearly weather-tight shelter by arranging a space between some of the cotton bales on which the skiff was tied. He and the woman whose child he'd saved, a young widow named Claudia, sat and watched the little boy playing on the small, dry patch of deck, oblivious to the storm.

Potut decided that they could stay, for now, but everything else on deck would have to go. Balks of Lebanese cedar, bags of dates and peppers, and bales of Egyptian cotton, all were consigned to Poseidon.

When the task was done the deck looked naked and, in fact, was more treacherous to try to cross. Potut ordered that every available line be strung as handholds about the deck, after which some of the passengers moved into the rope locker. A couple passengers joined Otho and Claudia. The other passengers squeezed into the hold. With no cargo on deck, every wave that broke over the bow rolled almost unimpeded for half the length of the deck before draining from the scuppers. The deck was unsafe for anyone other than the crew. Potut didn't see any passengers risk the crossing to the heads; the hold must be starting to stink.

The carpenter pondered the task he'd been given. The captain had asked for a hundred buckets, he would give him a hundred buckets. He hauled the mainsail on deck and began cutting it into pieces. Then he passed out bone needles and twine to several of the crewmen and they stitched the linen squares into buckets. A coating of lard was rubbed into the finished linen bags to improve their water-holding ability. The passengers who came up with loads of bilge water had to time their movements to the waves and even then, they only poked their heads up far enough to empty their bailers and dropped down again. By nightfall the passengers had lowered the level of water in the bilge to less than a cubit. The hungry passengers fell into exhausted sleep that even the storm couldn't disturb.

***

THERE WAS NO SUNRISE, only an easing of the blackness to announce the arrival of a new day. The storm raged unabated. As daylight grew, Potut could see the deck writhing

91

like a snake. The carpenter reported that the bilge water was back to nearly three cubits.

"Get the bailing started again." The carpenter set off the wake the sore, hungry passengers.

Potut found Abu asleep. He'd never seen Abu asleep before. The man had a knack for knowing when his captain needed him. He had to have been beyond exhausted to allow the captain to catch him sleeping. Potut decided to let him sleep. He turned instead to Julius.

"We are going to send the main mast overboard, also the derricks, and all the spars and spare timbers. Can your man Otho swing an axe?"

"Of course."

Julius had never actually seen Otho swing an axe, but he had never set the man any physical task that he'd been unable to accomplish. He called him over, and the captain explained what he wanted. Otho simply nodded and walked away. He had by now become familiar with the layout of the ship and he returned quickly with an axe. He laid into the mast, timing his strokes so that he could grab a handhold as needed when the ship swooped and fell. If anyone was sorry to see the ship abused in this fashion, no one said so aloud. Survival was all.

While Otho swung the axe Potut dispatched several crewmen to the stays that held the mast upright. It became a race between sailors untying or simply cutting lines and Otho chopping at the mast. Before the sailors had parted the last stay, a loud crack told the tale. Otho jumped back, and the mast, held precariously aloft by the single stay running to the starboard rail shivered, split, then fell over the starboard side. The sailor waiting at the stay quickly sliced through it. Otho looked over to Potut, who nodded his thanks, then pointed at the two derricks that were used to hoist cargo in and out of the holds. Otho shouldered the axe and headed for the nearest derrick.

CHAPTER 15

I REACHED THE STERN A MILLISECOND ahead of the flames and dove into the sea. It was weird being in the water at night but, thanks to the flames of the boat, it wasn't completely dark. I swam underwater away from the flames before I turned my face away from the boat and surfaced for a breath. If someone was watching, I didn't want them to spot the light reflecting on my face and discover they'd failed to kill me, assuming that was their plan. I ducked down again and, staying underwater, angled for the beach to the north of the boat.

I made it to shore on that breath and, staying as low as possible, I crawled out of the surf into the shadow of some sea grass and eeled through it. The sea grass was sharp and spine-covered, and I felt it slashing at my bare skin as I crawled, but I didn't care. I was sure now that a car had stopped and I was eager to catch whoever was driving it. I was getting sick and tired of this nonsense. What had I done to make someone want me dead? I had no weapons, but if I caught the guy I'd strangle him with my bare hands.

I could see a vague outline of a car on the road and I moved toward it. Before I got within twenty feet, however, I heard the door slam and the engine race. I jumped up and ran toward the car, the pavement cutting into my bare feet. But it accelerated quickly away to the north. By the time the driver turned his headlights on it was too far away for me to even read the license plate. I had only a vague impression of a midsized light colored sedan. Probably not more than a few thousand of those on the island.

Caroline came running up, wearing only a T-shirt and flip-flops. She was screaming.

"David! David!"

"I'm fine," I called back, and she turned and ran to where I was limping back from the road. She threw her arms around me and kissed me savagely.

"I thought I'd lost you."

"I'm fine; no harm, no foul. Missed the guy, though."

She had been awakened by the muffled explosion and looked out her bedroom window and seen the flames. She had lingered just long enough to call 112 and throw on some shoes.

We made quite a pair, standing on the beach in our underwear, staring at the burning boat, trying to keep each other warm.

"Oh, David! What can we do?"

I didn't see how we could do anything. In the distance I could hear a siren, but whether it was a cop or a fire truck wouldn't matter. The boat was now about thirty feet offshore and the flames were shooting several yards into the air. "We can't reach it, and even if we could we'd never get on board to use the extinguisher," I replied. "Maybe the emergency responders will be able to do something." But I knew they wouldn't.

"How did it get so far offshore?" Caroline asked.

"Good question." I walked back up the beach to where the anchor was dug in. Had the anchor rope burned through? The anchor was still there, with a couple feet of rope attached to it. I picked the rope up so Caroline could see the end of it in the firelight. "It's been cut."

"You don't think..." she gestured to the mosque. She didn't need to finish. As angry as the man from the mosque had been earlier in the day – yesterday, now – I wouldn't have been at all surprised to learn he had burned the boat and set it adrift.

"Could be, but there was someone in a car, and that guy," I gestured toward the mosque across the road, "wouldn't have needed

94

to drive here."

We'd been watching and listening to the progress of a fire truck. It slowed and drove onto the sand and men jumped off it wearing helmets and overcoats with reflective stripes. They quickly laid out a hose and then waded as far as they could into the surf and trained the hose upward, trying to arc the spray out onto the flames. But only a little of the water reached the boat. One of the men handed Caroline and I a blanket that we gratefully wrapped around ourselves. We thanked him and I asked if he could send for a policeman. He got on his radio and a minute later he let me know that someone was already on the way.

When a policeman arrived, I told him about the car and we showed him the cut anchor rope. Caroline and I took turns telling him about the confrontation with the fellow from the mosque. The cop, a short, stocky, no-nonsense bull of a man who had introduced himself as Superintendent Drago went straight across the road to the mosque and pounded on the front door. Caroline and I stayed put and watched the fire dwindle. After a few minutes Drago returned.

"The man who confronted you was one of the mullahs," Drago informed us. "He and two others live there at the mosque, along with the Imam. I spoke with the Imam, who claimed that he witnessed the confrontation you had earlier, and he chastised the mullah. He says the young man has been locked in his room all evening. The Imam was awakened by a noise and saw the light from the fire, but didn't see anyone or anything."

"Did you speak with the others?"

"No. The Imam assured me they didn't see anything, either." He shrugged. "Malta is 99 percent Catholic. Muslims are not generally popular, and they know it. They tend to keep to themselves."

I couldn't help wondering if someone was lying, but since there seemed to be no other witnesses, we'd never know.

With a hiss and a gurgle, the boat sank. I knew the depth where it went down was about ten or fifteen feet. Without the flames, we were left with only the lights from the firemen, who were preparing to leave, and the headlights of the Superintendent's car. "There's nothing more we can do here," he said. "Come by the stationhouse tomorrow and I'll take your statement."

As he headed to his car and we turned to walk back to Caroline's another car came rapidly down the coast road and pulled over. A disheveled and very agitated Anthony jumped out and ran to meet us.

"Superintendent Drago! Thank you for taking care of my friends! David, Caroline, are you all right?" Drago simply waved at Anthony and U-turned back to town, probably not wanting to lose any more sleep answering questions for Anthony.

"We're fine, Anthony. We weren't on board." It wasn't the time to explain my near-miss. "I'm sorry about your boat, though. Do you have insurance?"

"Don't worry about that now," he said. I took that for a No. The boat, I'd come to learn, was an old war surplus metal hull that had had several rebuilds in its long life, the last one adding a wood-paneled fiberglass inner hull and lockers, and a compartment covering a relatively new Chevy 350 inboard engine.

Anthony pressed on. "What about your belongings? Did you lose anything valuable?"

That struck me as an odd question. "Well, the detector and my new camera are both waterproof. If they didn't burn they should be okay. I'll dive down tomorrow and see what I can salvage. But there were no artifacts on board, no."

"Good, good. Well, the main thing is that you're okay. When I heard about the fire I was devastated that you might have been harmed." He pulled both of us into a hug, then took his leave.

***

WE SLOGGED, SHIVERING, to Caroline's. Back in the kitchen we'd so recently vacated, we were both too wired to get back to sleep. She went off to her room for a minute and came back wearing sweatpants. She'd also found a sweatshirt and a pair of shorts baggy enough to fit me. We held a pow-wow over brandy.

"So," I said. "Obviously someone wants me dead. Cutting the painter means what? Perhaps they were hoping the boat would drift away and no one would ever know what happened to me?"

"That doesn't seem likely," Caroline replied. "There was not

96

enough movement for the boat to drift away. They had to know the flames would be seen and the fire department would be called. I think it's more likely they wanted exactly what they got: that the boat would drift too far from shore to be put out easily, and then sink, ruining any evidence."

"That makes sense. Tomorrow I'll dive down and see what I can find."

"Have you thought," she added, "since this was an obvious attempt on your life, that maybe it wasn't just a drunk driver who ran you and Vito off the road the other night? One could be an accident, but not two."

"Three." I told her about the sabotaged weight belts and buoyancy compensators.

"David! Did you report that to the police?"

"Anthony seemed reluctant to involve them."

"He will have to change his mind now. So, who could be trying to kill you?"

"I have no idea. I haven't met that many people here."

"Why don't you name them all, we'll see if anyone stands out."

"Well, aside from waiters and shopkeepers, only a handful. Elvis and what's-his-name at the museum, Luca. I think we can rule out Elvis. I don't know anything about Luca, but I can't imagine what he'd gain from trying to kill me."

"I know Luca, he's harmless."

"You know Luca?"

"It's a small place. Who else?"

"Well, Anthony."

"Anthony didn't break into his own shop."

"No. And he would never do anything that would harm Vito."

"Exactly, so why did you even mention him?"

"Out at the beach just now, for just a second, he seemed surprised to see me. And, we know he has some secrets of some kind in the dive shop. Remember how he didn't want us calling the police after the break-in? And a few days ago he was asking about my sleeping arrangements."

"Why?"

"He thought I was sleeping with you and he wanted his room

97

back." Caroline blushed at this, and I probably did, too. "He said the priest had been asking where I was, because the good Father was wanting to use the back room for one of his assignations."

"So, Father Jim knew also."

"Actually, he's a better candidate than Anthony. He knows diving. He took an instant dislike to me because I wouldn't call him 'Father,' but that's a poor reason to try to kill someone. And even if he did take aim at me and Vito on the scooter, he's one of Anthony's 'Very Good Friends,' so I can't imagine him wrecking the dive shop or blowing up the boat."

"I agree, he wouldn't try to kill you for disrespecting him. And as for his secret liaisons, you know less about them than almost everyone else on the island. If he were willing to kill to keep them secret we'd all be dead."

"As for Anthony, I suspect tomorrow I'll find that he doesn't have insurance on his boat. Of course I plan to take care of it but he can't know that for sure... I could just as easily be a typical ugly American and jump on the next plane back to Phoenix and he'd be out one boat."

Caroline frowned when I mentioned going back to Phoenix. But then she had another idea. "What if Anthony has gotten involved with some bad people, like mafia? Perhaps they broke into his shop, they burned his boat? They could be looking for something, or they could simply be trying to cost him money or send him a message."

I turned that over in my head. "Good idea," I said. "But it doesn't explain someone trying to run me off the road, or the sabotage to the dive gear."

"Not everything is about you," she said with a smile. "Vito was run off the road, and Vito was involved in the diving mishap. Maybe someone was threatening Vito to get to Anthony."

I hadn't thought of that. I replayed all the scenarios with Vito in the lead role instead of me. It didn't wash.

"Possible. But there was no reason to think Vito was on the boat tonight. And whoever broke into the dive shop knew it was empty. The timing was too perfect. And hardly anything was taken. Seems like mafia goons would have come when Anthony was there, or would at least have cleaned out the shop once they broke in."

"Perhaps that was just an unconnected burglary and the burglars got scared off?"

"Whoever did it was not there to steal. After Anthony cleaned up I asked him what was missing and he said one Breitling dive watch. Everything else was there, just messed up. He believes it was just some kids up to no good. If they were there to steal, most of his dive watches and any of his regulators were worth more than my laptop. I think they came specifically to sabotage the dive gear. Then they took my laptop and my camera and his watch just to make it look like a robbery."

"Maybe your laptop and camera were the target. Was there anything special about them? Perhaps the pictures of the artifacts you'd found?"

"The laptop I've had for a while. I suppose it has some of my business stuff on it, the social security numbers and addresses and so on of my employees. That would be worth something to an identity thief. Problem with that is, without my password that laptop is as useless as a paperweight."

"What about the camera?"

"I got it new for this trip. And yes, it did have pictures of the mast cap, some of the coins, and the medallion. But why steal the pictures when you could just as easily steal the stuff? Some of the coins were in my room, right on the table next to the laptop, and they weren't touched."

Clearly, she and I were never going to be mistaken for Nancy Drew and the Hardy boys. We sat in companionable silence and sipped our brandy for a while.

"So, not Elvis, not Luca, not Anthony, not Father Jim. If it's mafia they are bunglers, and the mafia are not bunglers. Who does that leave?" Caroline asked. "Me?"

I grinned. "I suppose you could have been driving the car that ran Vito and me off the road. But Vito was under the impression that the driver was a man. I've seen you in a bikini, ma'am, and I don't think he would have mistaken you for a man."

"And I have a pretty good alibi for the dive shop break-in and burning the boat." She smiled.

"So that leaves just the mullah."

"He was certainly angry enough." She ticked items off on her fingers. "We know he already knew who you were when the car tried to hit you and Vito. Anthony had already shown him the *kilij* and told him who it came from. So that could have been him."

She ticked a second finger. "He was under the impression you had found more 'Muslim old things,' as he called them, so he could have broken into the dive shop looking for them."

Third finger. "Obviously, he had access to the boat tonight. He may have wanted you dead, or he may have simply wanted to burn the boat and scare you off."

I thought back to that firebomb arcing through the night sky. The difference between living and dying had been inches. That wasn't just a scare tactic. Someone had wanted me dead. I unconsciously rubbed my right forearm, where I discovered the hair was singed. Caroline noticed.

"Are you hurt?"

"No, I'm fine, just thinking. Whoever sabotaged the dive gear knew about scuba diving."

"True. We don't know that the mullah knows anything about diving. But we don't know that he doesn't, either. And he was so angry, so irrational. It had to be him."

"We'll never prove it. For that matter," I said, "if we have to consider motives as weird as that mullah thinking I'm stealing artifacts from his mosque, then 'Father' Jim could have some weird motive like thinking it will hurt the church if I prove that Paul's shipwreck didn't happen in Saint Paul's Bay."

"Or Elvis thinking it would harm the museum, or tourism. Either idea is too far-fetched."

"If someone was only trying to scare me," I said, "tonight's attack went too far. But if they wanted me dead, the earlier attacks didn't go far enough. I can't decide whether someone wants me dead, wants me to go away, or wants something I have. Until we know that, we aren't going to narrow down the list of suspects."

We finished our brandy. "Well," she said, "Thank you for defending my honor to Anthony. Unnecessary, but gallant."

"Sorry if I've besmirched your reputation. I'll be sure to tell Anthony tomorrow about using your spare room."

"It's a small island. If privacy is important to someone, they should not live here. My reputation can take care of itself – my conscience is clear. I'm happy you're here, and safe."

On that pleasant note, we headed for our respective beds.

***

WHEN I WOKE UP Caroline was gone. She'd laid out a pair of flip-flops next to the baggy sweatshirt. A note on the kitchen table told me that she would be back in time to drive me to a meeting she'd arranged with the director at 2:00.

Well, that wasn't going to work. A few things had clarified for me while I'd slept. I found a dusty mask and snorkel hanging on a hook on the back porch and walked to the beach.

I dropped a towel and my shirt on the sand, stepped out of the shorts and waded into the ocean in my underwear. It was as still as a millpond, and I could see the boat sitting upright on the bottom. The first dive down I just looked at it. The wood was charred, the fiberglass was misshapen, and most of the upholstery was gone. The ocean floor around the wreck was littered with what might once have been my swim trunks, some charts and other light stuff that had partially survived the fire then drifted away during the night.

The boat had gone down so smoothly, however, that the heavier stuff was still where it had been when I'd left the boat in a hurry the night before. I had locked the dive equipment in the locker under the bow, but a boathook and some of Anthony's fishing poles still lay scattered about the deck.

Also on the deck were some broken shards of brown glass. I returned to the surface for a breath, then swam closer to a piece of the glass that had a recognizable shape. It was the neck of a bottle with a loop for a handle and, more importantly, a metal label that looked like it might be readable in good light. I didn't know what it was, but I knew it hadn't been on board the day before.

I grabbed the remnants of my jeans from where they lay on the deck and went up for another breath. They were about half burned, but my keys were still lodged in the right front pocket. I worked them out and let go of the burnt jeans, got the right key ready in my hand, and dove again. The key fit easily into the lock, but the locker door was warped, and it took three strong tugs to get it open. The contents seemed to be mostly intact. I grabbed my camera and my dive bag, jammed the locker shut again and pushed off toward the surface. When my breathing calmed, I turned on the camera and dove again. I took several pictures of the whole mess. On successive dives I swam down both sides of the entire hull to see if the fire had injured the metal. Thankfully, the only holes I found were the ones that were supposed to be there: two drains, their plugs now melted away; the prop shaft, probably encased in the melted remains of a burned-up bushing; a small hole where a sonar transducer had been; and two large holes that allowed water to circulate through the engine for cooling.

After treading water on the surface for a while I went down one more time. This trip I carefully collected the largest pieces of the broken brown glass into my dive bag, and I was done.

After I toweled off and put my clothes on I wrapped the snorkel and mask in the towel and wedged them under the anchor that was still buried in the sea grass. I started hiking up the road to town. I'd seen Vito do it several times, it wouldn't kill me to make the long walk once. Of course Vito didn't do it wearing too-small flip-flops and wet underwear...

***

"AH, *SAVINA LARINGINA*." Superintendent Drago recognized the label before it was even close enough to read. "A very popular liqueur here. Do you like it?"

At the police station I had carefully removed the bottle fragments from my dive bag and was laying them out on Superintendent Drago's desk.

"I wouldn't know, I've never tried it. The only glass we had on the boat was a beer bottle or two. If you can figure out who broke this on the boat, you'll know who's trying to kill me."

Superintendent Drago gave me a stern look for suggesting that such a crime would be contemplated in his pleasant little town. "I'm sure no one was trying to kill you. Besides, *Savina Laringina* is a liqueur, not hard spirits. It would not start a fire."

"Okay, but something did. This bottle was not on board when I went to sleep, but the pieces were there this morning when I dove to the wreck. I think someone filled this with gasoline, stuffed a rag in the neck and lit it, and threw it onto the boat."

"A Molotov cocktail."

"Exactly. The same mystery guest then cut the anchor rope. You might consider this simply as mischief, Superintendent, but if I'd been sound asleep on that boat as I was supposed to have been, you would be spending today investigating not just the loss of Anthony's boat but the loss of an American tourist and one of Anthony's Very Good Friends." I wasn't sure how much clout the 'Anthony's friends' club had, but I figured I might as well remind the Superintendent that I was a member.

The Superintendent nodded and pulled on some rubber gloves. "So, Anthony's friend, we will do the *CSI*, yes?"

He carefully lifted some of the shards and carried them to another room. It took him three trips. One of the other officers sitting at a nearby desk saw him and smirked, shaking his head. I heard him mumble something about Horatio Caine, the red-haired cop on *CSI Miami*, and another officer laughed at the remark. Who knew the show had fans in Malta? Apparently Drago's fellow officers had seen him go through this routine before. I decided to join Drago.

The small room behind the main bull pen had no windows. It looked like it may have started life as a cell or a large closet.

"This used to be full of file cabinets," he saw me looking at the small room. "Since all the files were put on the computer we turned it into our crime lab." He smiled when he said it. He knew it wasn't much of a lab.

On a counter against one wall was what looked suspiciously like an aquarium, empty of water, propped up on, was that a bicycle basket? The empty aquarium held the broken glass pieces and a small coffee cup. Drago was adding the last two pieces of the orange liqueur bottle into the aquarium. He stepped across the room and grabbed a tea kettle off a hotplate and poured some hot water into the coffee cup in the aquarium. He dug around in the garbage can and came up with a soda can. Using his pocket knife he cut the can in half, then

103

picked up a tube of super glue and squeezed a dime-sized dollop into the bottom of the can and placed it into the aquarium. He covered the aquarium with a piece of cardboard with a hole in its center, and turned on an exhaust fan set into the wall above the whole apparatus. Lastly, he turned back to the other wall, unplugged the hotplate and brought it over and stuck it in the bicycle basket under the aquarium, and plugged it back in.

"Now we wait. I've surprised you, yes? You did not expect us to have this technology, did you?" What was he calling technology: the aquarium, the hotplate or the super glue?

"You've surprised me, yes. I've seen this on TV. The superglue evaporates and the fumes stick to the fingerprints, if there are any, right?"

"Precisely!"

"What's the hot water for?"

"The process works better with higher humidity. Malta is very dry."

"How long does it take?"

"Oh, it is nothing like the *CSI* show. If there are any usable fingerprints I'll have them by the end of the day. But finding out if they match anyone, that will take much longer. We will see what we will see."

***

DRAGO HAD BEEN KIND enough to let me use the telephone and directory in an office and leave the room so I had some privacy. I first called Caroline and asked her to cancel the meeting with the director.

"Certainly, if you wish. But why?"

"Two reasons. One, I collected proof the boat fire wasn't an accident. Superintendent Drago is working on it now. And I haven't even begun working on the boat."

"I understand. I can go to the meeting without you."

"You could, but I'd rather you didn't."

She paused for a moment. "Why not?" She sounded skeptical. Did she still think I was a treasure hunter?

104

"My second reason. You promised me a day, for just us."

She understood what I meant. "But you have no boat now. How can we dive the site?"

"I'll get another boat. I want that one dive day. It won't be today, might not be for a few days yet, but I want that day. Okay?"

"Certainly, David. Those amphorae have lain there for centuries, a few more days won't hurt. Will I see you for dinner?"

"Not tonight. I have too much to do. I'll be in touch." I rang off. I knew she was disappointed, but I couldn't let that sway me. If someone really was trying to kill me, I didn't want Caroline caught in the crossfire. The shards of glass from the Molotov cocktail were a grim reminder that this whole business was getting serious.

Using Drago's directory and phone I quickly learned that buying Anthony a new dive boat would not only end my vacation, it would cancel my vacations for years. I called the only marine salvage operation listed in the yellow pages. They already knew about the fire, and told me what they would charge to raise the boat – nearly a quarter of what it would cost to buy new one. I had to come up with another plan.

Following Drago's directions I found a hardware store and made some purchases. Then I hired a tow truck, and made sure he had a long cable. I rode with the driver out to the beach and directed the driver where to put his truck, with the back end toward the water. While he unwound all his cable I retrieved my mask and snorkel. By now my underwear was dry, just in time to get wet again. Too bad my swim trunks had burned. Too bad I didn't think to buy some when I was in town!

I stripped down, put on the mask and waded into the water carrying the hook on the end of the tow truck's cable. I took a breath and dove to the boat. After I attached the cable to the bow eye of Anthony's sad looking boat I surfaced and gave a thumbs-up to the tow truck driver. I treaded water while he worked a lever on the side of his truck and began winching in the cable. I watched through the mask as the line came tight, then the boat began sliding over the bottom. I looked back to the tow truck and it wasn't even straining. This might work!

The tow truck driver stopped when the boat's awning broke

the surface. I signaled him to continue slowly, then I stopped him when the side rails were a few inches above sea level. He backed the winch to put some slack into the line and I disconnected it. As he spooled it up I came out of the water long enough to give him a damp tip, and sent him on his way.

From the hardware store bag I pulled out some quick-curing underwater sealant and a battery powered bilge pump. Back in the water I dove down at the stern of the boat and applied the sealant to the holes where the drain plugs had melted away, and smeared as much as I could around the prop shaft. Over several trips I crammed pieces of my burnt swim trunks and jeans into the engine water intakes, then gooped all the remaining sealant over the rags.

I pried open the engine cover and set up the battery operated pump in the lowest point of the bilge that I could reach, and ran the output hose over the side. As an afterthought, I optimistically tied a new painter from the bow eye to the anchor stuck in the beach, then dressed and walked back to Caroline's. I threw my clothes in her washing machine and took a shower. After the shower I moved my laundry to the dryer and made myself a sandwich – if anyone had walked in and found me naked in Caroline's kitchen making a sandwich I don't think any explanation would have sufficed, but no one did.

While I ate, I looked at the goodies we'd found so far. The amphora was missing. Caroline would have taken it to show to the director. I hoped she would keep her word and leave him in the dark for now. I wanted to make the case to the director myself.

I peeked in on the medallion where it lay soaking. It looked good. That one word was definitely 'phylake' and the next word looked like 'sou.' I lifted it out of the basin and scrubbed at it with a toothbrush Caroline had left there for that purpose. The last of the scale came off in a clump, and I saw the whole medallion almost as if it had just been made.

I spent the next hour translating the entire Greek text. As I worked, as the text became clear, so did my future. When I was done, I knew how I was going to pay for the repairs to Anthony's boat.

106

CHAPTER 16

WITH THE MAINMAST AND DERRICKS gone and the deck nearly empty, the ship looked like a hulk. The foresail yard was stowed below. All that interrupted the expanse of the deck, besides the crew cabin on the bow and the captain's cabin near the stern, was the naked foremast, looking like a flagpole on a parade ground, and the cotton bale/skiff shelter Otho had constructed for Claudia and her child. One way or another, this would be the ship's last voyage. But she was no longer twisting like a serpent, and shortly the carpenter came to report that they were finally making headway against the bilge water. Potut simply nodded his acknowledgement as if it was exactly what he had expected. In fact, it was really excellent news, but Potut couldn't allow the men to see his relief. That would imply that he'd been worried. Besides, they still had a long way to go.

Abu came scurrying aft, as if embarrassed that he'd needed any sleep. His captain didn't mention it, just got right to business.

"The carpenter tells me the level in the bilge is dropping. Arrange the passengers into four crews, two for the day and two for night. Some can get some rest while others bail. Set two men on each steering oar, and the rest of the crew to every task you can find that will tighten up the ship, even a little."

"The wheat?"

107

"Keep the wheat, for now. Who knows? Perhaps the gods will allow us to salvage something from this trip. If we get in trouble, we'll toss it."

"Very good, sir."

As Abu started to turn away the captain stopped him. "Abu. Don't push them too hard, the passengers. They are exhausted. So is the crew for that matter. Make sure each man gets some sleep. And you get some, too."

"Yes sir."

***

THE DAYS AND NIGHTS blurred into one another. The storm refused to relent. To most of the 276 people on board, it was as if the entire universe had shrunk to only the wind, the waves, the noise, and the motion.

Every few dozen waves – or few hundred, what difference did it make? – a rogue wave came, larger, or from a different angle, and crashed over the ship's bow, rolling nearly to the stern. Water would pour in around the edges of the hatch covers. The wooden structure would shriek and work, the bands tied around the hull amidships like the corset of a harlot would stretch and threaten to break, then go slack and flap on the deck. And the steersmen at the steering oars, tied to deck rings by lines around their ankles, would make signs to their gods and hold their breath. The unending waves and the working of the ship let more water into the bilge, and the passengers heaved the water out again in a never-ending cycle.

Other than the crew, no one but Otho and his de facto family dared venture on deck, even to ease nature. The atmosphere in the hold was a fetid conglomeration of human and animal stench, waste, vomit and mildew, and Otho preferred the occasional soaking in the fresh air to living in what he was sure were diseased conditions below. Claudia was convinced her life, and the life of her child, were secure as long as she stayed beside the giant.

Below decks, anything that wasn't sealed in an amphora

108

was soaked through. Salt-soaked clothing rubbed skin until it bled; salt-stiffened hair stuck out like bristles on the snout of a pig; blisters broke and suppurated; salt had reddened every eye on board until the passengers looked like mourners at a funeral.

They weren't going to make it, Potut decided. They had to take more drastic action. He approached Otho's makeshift shelter.

"I'm afraid I'm going to have to send you below. I'm going to get rid of these cotton bales and set the skiff flat on the deck. If it's any consolation, I'm sending the cabins overboard as well. Before I do, I need you to bring the prisoner Demetrius to me."

If Otho thought this was a strange request he said nothing. He took Claudia and her child below, and returned a few moments later with a whining Demetrius in tow.

"You have no right! I'll die on deck! Let go of me!" Otho shoved Demetrius into the captain's cabin and withdrew. Demetrius flew in and splayed on the floor next to the captain's bunk. Potut looked down at him, waiting until the man was squirming under his gaze. Then he spoke.

"I've come to a conclusion about you," the captain said. "You value your life more than anyone else on board this ship. I, on the other hand, place less value on your life than on one of the chickens or goats. Less than the smallest, meanest rat in the bilge. I could throw you overboard and call it an offering to the gods and it would trouble me not at all. Do you understand what I'm saying?"

"Why would you do that? What have I done?"

"I have no idea what you've done. I'm sure you've done plenty. And I don't care. I'm trying to impress on you that I care not one whit whether you live or die. Am I clear so far? A Yes or No is all I need."

"Yes."

"Good." Potut reached under his bunk and pulled out the lead-encased box. "My cabin, and therefore my bunk, is going overboard. So I no longer have a secure place for this."

"What is it?"

109

"You don't need to know that. What you do need to know is that it represents your life." Potut paused to let that thought sink in. "Your life, Demetrius. Right here in this box."

He tossed the box into Demetrius' lap. "I'm sure by now you have carved out a niche for yourself on my ship, wherever you consider safest. And I'm sure you are right; wherever it is will be the safest place on board; you have an instinct for self-preservation. You will hide this box there, where no one will find it. Every day at first light, from now until we reach Italy, you will come find me and show me the box."

Demetrius started to object but Potut talked over him. "If you fail to show up, I will instruct Otho or Abu to bring you to me. If you show up without the box, you go overboard. If the box doesn't look exactly as it does right now, if it has so much as a scratch on it, you will go overboard. No exceptions, no excuses. Is that clear?"

Demetrius couldn't drag his gaze from the box. He just nodded.

"Good! Abu tells me you have been no help with bailing." Abu hadn't said any such thing, but the guilty look from Demetrius told the captain he was right. "Well, now you have something useful to contribute – guarding this box with your life. I'll see you, and my box, tomorrow at first light. Dismissed."

The defrauder of widows scuttled out of the cabin with the lead-lined box clutched under an arm. A wave swept the deck at that moment and knocked him from his feet and Potut caught his breath. But the water receded, and he watched Demetrius rise dripping from the deck, still clutching the box, and hurry off toward the bow.

"Abu!"

The man must have been nearby, he appeared at once. "Yes, sir?"

Potut waved at all the goods packed into his cabin. "Throw it all overboard, then dismantle the cabin and get rid of it as well."

One alabaster case of nard, smaller than a wine bottle, was worth more than Abu received in six months, and there were dozens of them. Not to mention the sodden bundles of silk and cinnamon bark. But he didn't bat an eye at the order to destroy thousands of *denarii* worth of goods. He simply set to work.

CHAPTER 17

AFTER MY CLOTHES DRIED I carefully wrapped up the medallion and put it in my pocket. Scrounging around in Caroline's garage produced an old bicycle, and I pedaled back to the beach to check on the progress of the boat.

The boat was floating, but low in the water. It still had a ways to go. The bilge pump I'd purchased would shut itself off when the job was done, so I headed for town. I checked with Anthony about insurance – sure enough, he had none – then I set off to rent another boat.

I threw the bike on board the new boat and piloted it back to the beach where Anthony's boat, from a distance, was now looking almost normal. Up close, of course, was another story. The awning was nothing but a frame, and the entire upper surface of the bow was blackened, the fiberglass bent and bubbled. The old adage about boats being 'a hole in the water into which you throw money' was absolutely true. While I had dodged the cost of a new boat, it would still cost more than my whole vacation to get Anthony's boat rebuilt. I towed it back to Saint Paul's Bay, to the marina where I had rented the new boat and set them to work on it.

I thought about collecting Vito and going back to the dive site for the last couple hours of daylight. But the promise I'd extracted from Caroline cut both ways: 'one more day' of diving before the

History department took over, implied that I only got the one day. If I went now with Vito, Caroline might view that as my 'one day.' With what I now knew, I didn't want to waste my day; and I didn't want to risk losing Caroline's trust by going out without her. Besides, I was exhausted.

I docked the new boat at Anthony's just as he was locking up and I filled him in on my day. He was pleased I'd managed to salvage his boat and weakly objected to my plan to pay for the repairs, but I knew he would agree in the end. It was my responsibility after all, not his; and he loved money too much to just eat the cost himself in the name of Maltese hospitality or customer satisfaction.

I tried calling the office in Arizona, but the call went straight to the answering service. That could be a good thing, I told myself. It could be that Gary was actually out in the field working on extinguishers. The guy that answered, who identified himself as Mario, had no idea why the office wasn't picking up.

"Maybe he's at lunch," Mario the unhelpful answering service guy advised me. It was only 11 a.m. in Phoenix, early for Gary to go to lunch. "Or maybe all the lines are in use." Or maybe Gary is just ducking my calls. I called Gary's cell but the call went straight to voicemail. Definitely ducking my calls.

If I sold the business to Metropolitan Gary would become their problem. If my relationship with Caroline fizzled, which still looked like a possibility, I'd keep the business but when I got home, I'd have to give serious thought to replacing Gary. It's never a good idea to hire relatives.

I changed clothes in my little room, transferring the medallion to my jeans, then locked the shop and went to dinner. As far as I could tell, no one tried to kill me the rest of the evening.

***

THE NEXT DAY, I was at loose ends. No diving the site until Caroline was free, and she had classes all day. So it would be another day at least before we got the promised day of diving the site together. What to do with myself?

I'd read on the internet about some Roman-era anchors on

display at the Maritime Museum about a half hour south of Saint Paul's Bay, in a suburb of Valetta called Birgu. Well, probably more like an hour by rental Vespa. I took an inland road on which one town seemed to run right into the next. Malta was really crowded. It was also clear that the highway planners loved roundabouts. I went around a dozen of them on the short trip.

On the outskirts of Valetta I saw a familiar bright red and yellow sign – McDonald's! I made a note of it to stop for an American break on the way home. I continued south past the Marsa horse racing track and the Marsa Royal Golf course. In Paul's day, Marsa had been a bay, but over the centuries the bay had silted up, and now it was a country club. I watched a golfer shank a ball that bounced off a tree, off the road, and flew right over my head. I heard the car behind me slam on its brakes. The golfer waved his arms and threw his club. Just like home.

I found the museum, locked up the Vespa and paid my admission. The Maritime Museum was housed in a building that in Napoleon's day had been a bakery. The staple of sailors back then had been "ship's biscuit," bread baked hard as a rock and packed in (theoretically) air- and water-tight barrels; thus the navy had needed a bakery.

I wandered past displays that were undoubtedly of interest to British visitors. Several large, intricate models of sailing ships; figureheads from different centuries; a bronze cannon from the Siege of Malta; a French lieutenant's sabre from the Napoleonic era. A mural depicting the Siege of Malta showed an angel protecting the Catholic ships and devils surrounding the Saracens. I wondered if that mullah had seen this.

At last I came to my goal, the Roman anchors. I snapped a couple photos. I had read on the net that four had been found at the fifteen fathom line, not in Saint Paul's Bay but at the southeast end of the island, at a place called Saint Thomas Bay. However, the collection of anchors at the museum, dozens of them, said nothing about Paul's shipwreck. It said only that Malta had been a significant port for freighters going to and from Rome in the first century.

At least they had nothing that would contradict my findings. All that I needed to do now was to present the case for my site off 'Blast a

Giraffe' to someone authoritative in the academic world, like the department head, or even the president, of Caroline's college.

Assuming I survived the trip home. Thanks to the roundabouts I had spotted a dirty gray Ford Taurus following me from Saint Paul's Bay. It was the car that had had to brake to avoid losing its windshield to the errant golf ball. I had used the glass of the display cases at the museum to try to spot the reflection of whoever was following me, but I hadn't seen anyone. Either I wasn't very good at this, or whoever it was had opted to stay outside and watch for me to rejoin the Vespa, because the gray Taurus was again on my tail as I headed home.

I pulled into McDonald's and parked the bike. I was counting on the layout of this McDonald's being the same as every other McDonald's in the known universe, and it was. I walked in the front door, ordered some fries to go, then crossed the lobby and went out the door on the drive-through side. Once outside I quickly ducked through the cars waiting for take-out and ran around the back of the building.

The Taurus was parked under a tree on the far side of the parking lot. The driver had backed in, presumably so he could keep an eye on the Vespa. I snuck around behind the parking lot and approached him from behind. His window was down, his right elbow resting on the window frame. I could hear music coming from his radio. Staying out of the line of sight of the side-view mirror I ran up to his side of the car and opened the rear door.

The driver started to turn his head, but he wasn't fast enough. I was sick and tired of being hunted and I was determined to end it now.

I reached through the front window, grabbed the chain hanging around the driver's neck, and pulled it through the hinge-side opening of the rear door, then jumped in the back seat and slammed the door on the chain. The driver's head was pulled to his right and trapped back against the headrest. I could see the chain cutting into the wattles under his chin, and I could see his right eye bulging but it was fright, not suffocation.

"Forgive me 'Father' for I have sinned. Let's talk."

***

I RODE THE VESPA back to Saint Paul's Bay feeling better than I had in days. No one was trying to kill me anymore. I felt pretty good about my chances, not only with the plan I was going to present to the college, but with Caroline.

**

The conversation with 'Father' Jim had gone like this:

"I can't breathe!"

"Sure you can. It takes breath to talk, and you're talking just fine." I reached into the front and removed his dog collar and unbuttoned the top button of his shirt.

"What are you doing?" he yelled.

"Relax, you said you couldn't breathe, I'm just helping out." In reality, I'd belatedly remembered that Malta was almost entirely Catholic, and it occurred to me that someone passing by might object to my mistreating a priest. "Now, since we're going to be here awhile, why don't you explain to me why you've been trying to kill me?"

"You're crazy! I'm not trying to kill you! You're trying to kill me! If you don't let me go, I'm going to start screaming!"

"You're not going to start screaming. You have good reason not to call attention to yourself."

I didn't know exactly what those reasons were, but something had made him come after me. "You've tried to kill me three times." I itemized them for him. "You ran me and Vito off the road the other night. You sabotaged our diving gear. And you blew up Anthony's boat when I was sleeping on it."

"I don't know what you're talking about! I did none of those things!"

"Keep your voice down. Superintendent Drago found your fingerprints." That reminded me, it was probably time to check back with Drago to see if he had actually found any usable prints.

"Impossible! I haven't done anything wrong!"

"Vito saw you behind the wheel when you ran us off the road."

That shut him up. After a beat he said, with much less bluster. "I would never hurt Vito. And he's fine, I checked afterward with

116

Anthony."

"'Afterward?' After what? After you ran us off the road, you mean. So, again, why are you trying to kill me? Or are you trying to kill Vito?"

"Please! I would never harm Vito, I tell you! He's a beautiful boy. If you would just mind your own business..."

"Okay, now we're getting somewhere. You were trying to kill me, not Vito. I suppose that explains blowing up the boat, but you're forgetting messing with the buoyancy compensators and weights. Vito could easily have drowned because of you."

"I swear I don't know what you're talking about. Yes, I bumped your Vespa on the *Triq Il Kosta*, but I wasn't trying to hurt Vito. I just thought I could... I don't know what I thought. I was just so mad that you took my picture, and I wasn't thinking clearly."

With an almost audible Click, several things fell into place.

"So, you knew I was staying in the back room in Anthony's dive shop, and you broke in there to steal my camera. You messed the place up to make it look like a burglary." He didn't say anything, but his non-denial spoke volumes. I reached over the seat and grabbed his left arm and pulled up his sleeve. His watch was a cheap, flashy Casio, not Anthony's missing Breitling. "You can protest your innocence all you like, it was all my fault, blah, blah, blah, but you couldn't resist taking a two thousand dollar watch. That was just greed. It must be killing you that you can't wear it until Anthony forgets about it. It makes me wonder what other trouble your greed has gotten you into."

I unbuckled his Casio and dropped it into my McDonald's bag. It had some nice shiny surfaces Drago might be able to work with. Hmm, maybe not enough. I pulled off his sunglasses, dangled them where he could reach them and after he grabbed at them with both hands I pulled them from his grasp and dropped them in the bag as well.

"Those are mine! You can't just steal my things!"

"The crime is terrible in this country. You should report me to the authorities." Once Drago ran the prints, I suspected the good Father would have more to worry about than stealing Anthony's watch or my laptop. "Anthony reported the break-in, you know. Drago fingerprinted everything, and I'm sure he'll be able to match your prints on the watch and the sunglasses with the prints he lifted from Anthony's."

"Okay, I broke Anthony's door. And I trashed the shop to cover up taking your camera and laptop. But I was going to find a way to make it up to Anthony, I swear."

"Sure you were." Wait a minute, what did he just say? "Why did you take my laptop?"

He sat in silence for a bit, while his face got redder. The truth finally exploded out of him. "Because you said you were going to put my picture on Facebook! I couldn't let you do that."

That was the missing piece of the puzzle. "You've been a naughty boy, haven't you, James?" No reply. "What was it – did you get exposed on *'To Catch a Predator'*? Had to be something like that. And the Church moved you far away to Malta so you could continue to prey on young girls?" Still no response. No, wait. "Young boys?" His whole weight sagged against the chain, and I started to worry that he would choke, or maybe have a heart attack. But he finally straightened himself up and drew a breath.

"The Church didn't move me, they don't know. Running away was, something I did on my own."

"Why would you do that?"

"Because a man in Iowa was planning to kill me."

"Again, why?"

"He... he caught me with his son. Jamieson... well, he totally misunderstood, Jamieson and I had a very special... anyway, Jamieson's father was completely insane! He was going to murder me! Jamieson called and warned me. He overheard his father and mother talking about it, calmly discussing how much prison time his father would get if he pleaded insanity. Imagine!"

"Yeah, there's no justice. My heart bleeds for you. So then?"

"So, anyway, I got away and came here. I'd been to University here years ago and I always liked the place. I changed my name and forged some reassignment papers and showed up. The bishop didn't ask any questions, he was shorthanded. And then you came and messed it all up!"

"Where in Iowa?"

He paused, thinking. "Why do you need to know that?" I grabbed the chain between his neck and the doorpost and pulled on it. "Okay, Okay! Duncombe!"

"And Jamieson's last name?"

"Miller! Let go!"

"How old was Jamieson?"

"You're hurting me!"

"How old?"

"Fourteen!" I let go of the chain but kept it wedged in the door. I reached over the seat and removed the keys from the ignition, then clicked off my camera. "What was that? I heard a click."

"Oh, did I forget to mention it? Yeah, after you stole my camera I had to get a new one. Actually, you did me a favor. This new one can record nearly an hour of video."

I climbed out the left side and left him with his chain trapped in the right rear door. I was sure someone would let him loose eventually, and frankly I didn't particularly care if they did or not. I just hoped I could get my video to Drago before 'Father' Jim could get to the airport.

* * *

I CALLED ANTHONY and told him I was going to report an edited version of the break-in to Drago, and he reluctantly agreed. I went to the station and showed part of the video to Drago and gave him the McDonald's sack with the watch and sunglasses.

"You've been busy. I pulled a print off the broken bottle. So far, the computer has found no match to anyone in the system, but it is still searching. If I can get a print off the watch or glasses, and assuming they match, I'll pick up the Father and charge him with burglary and arson."

"Why not attempted murder?" I asked.

"Well, you weren't hurt."

"Not for lack of trying."

"It would be a difficult case to prove. Frankly, if the Father makes restitution to Anthony for the damage to his shop and his boat, there probably won't be any charges at all."

119

"But he's an admitted pedophile!"

"I have no evidence to charge him with child abuse here, and I have no jurisdiction in Iowa. However, I will check with the police there to see if they want to extradite him."

That was probably the best solution I was going to get. I headed to the museum to collect my mast cap.

***

LUCA WAS AGAIN manning the main desk of the little museum. After the conversation with Caroline about suspects, I felt silly for ever having suspected him. He acknowledged my presence, didn't seem surprised to see me unharmed. Nor did he look guilty of running me off the road or breaking into Anthony's shop. I'm no Sherlock Holmes. Maybe behind the dumb eyebrow ring and vacant marijuana-mellowed eyes lurked the mind of a master criminal. But after my conversation with the priest I figured I'd let Luca off the hook. He picked up the phone and summoned Elspeth/Elvis and after a minute she came bustling out.

But she was flustered. The ancient bronze mast cap was gone.

CHAPTER
18

ON THE DECK AT THE BOW, the cabin that had housed Julius, his guards, the off-duty crew and all their water jugs had been dismantled and had followed the captain's stern cabin over the side. In consequence, several amphorae of wheat in the hold had been tossed to make room for the water jugs, and Julius and Potut and the crew crammed themselves in below decks with all their men and the passengers. The weather was too extreme for anyone to survive even a short watch trying to hold on to one of the steering oars. The oars had been centered and lashed down as securely as possible, and the steersmen joined everyone else below. The seams of the hatches had been packed with linen to seal them, and the water coming in around them had been reduced to a drizzle.

The storm had grown so complete that Potut, when he had ventured on deck to check on the tillers, couldn't even guess where the sun was. A sunrise or sunset sighting would have given some reassurance of direction but there was none. Merely daylight, or the absence thereof. He assumed that north was roughly the direction from which the gale still, unrelentingly, blew, but that small piece of information was practically useless.

Noses had become immune to the stench, just as ears had become accustomed to the roar of wind and water; balance had adapted to the wild gyrations of the hold, and stomachs had become accustomed to emptiness. Children had stopped crying. Some slept, but others clung to their mothers and stared at nothing.

One of the passengers had gone berserk, screaming and clawing at the wax coated sailcloth covering the skylight that was the source of some dim light – and a constant drip – into the hold. It had taken several men to restrain him, and now he sat, whimpering every time the deck tilted too far for his liking, his hands and feet tied.

As the ship tossed, the circle sitting on the deck around Paul, Luke and Aristarchus continued to grow, as Paul taught them from his vast reserve of scriptural knowledge, memorized as a young Pharisee studying at the feet of the famous rabbi Gamaliel. He explained how Jesus of Nazareth had fulfilled Jewish prophecies of a coming messiah written down hundreds of years in advance; how he had introduced a new religion that required its adherents to put others ahead of themselves and God above all; why the man had subsequently been killed. He told them of his own history, how as a Pharisee he had zealously persecuted and killed Christians until Jesus had appeared to him in a blinding miracle and redirected his zeal. It was for that zeal that his Jewish former allies had had him arrested.

When the growing light indicated another day was beginning, an altercation broke out.

"We're all going to die!" a man screamed at Potut. Abu knocked the man down. Another man raised his voice and began trying to pull himself to his feet, but Otho glared at him, and the man sat back down again. Then Paul stood up.

"Men, friends. Had you taken my advice that we winter in Crete, we would not have sustained the damage and loss we have."

Potut snarled at him. "I don't need you to tell me how to sail my ship. Besides, Julius agreed!"

"I do not mention it to cause you humiliation, sir, merely to establish my credence. Just as my God gave me foreknowledge of the outcome while we were in Crete, this night his angel stood by me, saying, 'Have no fear, Paul. You will stand before Caesar. And God has graciously granted you the safety of all these sailing with you. You will lose the ship, but not a soul of you will be lost. You will all be cast upon an island.' So my advice now is that we lift our spirits. My God, to whom I have rendered sacred service these many years, will do exactly as he has promised. He will protect us."

Potut didn't care about Paul's god, but at least the speech had quieted the passengers. Several of those who hadn't paid Paul any attention before began asking him for more specifics about their future.

Two men took out tabula pieces and dice and set them on a game board they had carved into the cargo deck. A little girl put her doll in a wooden dish and swooped the dish up and down, mimicking the rise and fall of the ship. Some of the children chewed on some dried figs.

Almost against his will, Potut grudgingly found himself acknowledging that Paul had a power over these people greater than a captain's authority. Who knows, he thought. Maybe God did talk to him.

The carpenter approached and knuckled his brow. "Sir, the bilge is back over two cubits."

"Set a bailing crew. Let me know how long it takes to get it down to a cubit."

The carpenter acknowledged the order and headed off. Potut had already jettisoned a fortune in cargo. He hated to lose more, but he didn't want to lose his life when, if Paul were to be believed, the ordeal could be nearing its end.

CHAPTER 19

"DWEJRA CAME FOR the mast cap this morning. She said you and she were working together, so I thought it would be all right to give it to her. Was I wrong?"

I assured her it was fine, just poor communication on my part. "How is it progressing? Can you tell me anything else about it?"

"The mast cap is coming along quite nicely. Very similar in design to the Egyptian one in the catalog. There is some artwork on one side. The design is very early, possibly before Christ, but of course it could have been popular for several centuries after that. I was able to find only about a dozen similar examples in other collections, though there are also descriptions and drawings in contemporaneous literature..." She was running out of details. I could tell she felt she had messed up by giving my property away and was trying make up for it.

I thanked her for all her effort and told her either Caroline or I would be in touch. She looked puzzled until I said, "I mean Dwejra."

I walked along the sea wall. I'm sure there were tourists strolling along enjoying the sun and the view but I was not one of them. Walking had always helped me clear my head, and I powered along heedless of where I was going or what I was walking past.

The other night we had joked about Caroline's involvement in the plot. But today she had taken the ship artifact without telling me. Was it really possible she had an agenda that didn't include me, or was I being paranoid? A line from some movie swam into my head: 'It's amazing how an attempt on one's life focuses the mind.'

Did it make any sense that she would steal from me? No. She had left the medallion at the house. I was no expert, but I suspected that the value of the medallion would end up being more than an old piece of ship hardware. But that's just it: I was no expert.

But was it possible she could use the artifacts, in combination with the amphora handle she'd found, to advance her career? I had no idea. I was unfamiliar with the world of academia. I realized I didn't really know her that well. Perhaps her position at the college needed a boost. What if she was in competition with one of the other professors to produce some significant find in order to keep her job? Didn't college people have a slogan that ran 'Publish or perish'? Did she take the mast cap to claim credit for some major historical find?

Stop it, David. It may only have been a week or two, but in fact I did know her quite well. In fact, I felt like I'd known her all my life. If she had an ulterior motive, why would she have promised me a day of diving without scholastic interference?

Furthermore, I was clearly falling for her. And unless I was a complete idiot I was pretty sure she had feelings for me as well. I had avoided allowing myself to develop feelings for anyone for years. I'd been married once, briefly, and within weeks of saying 'I do' I had discovered the woman I'd married was not at all what she appeared. She was a pathological liar and a chameleon. She had transformed herself into what she knew I was looking for, but her true self had been nothing at all like the image she projected. Since then, my built-in lie detector was on full alert whenever I found myself attracted to a woman. And I'd gotten no bad vibes from Caroline.

So there had to be some other explanation.

***

"YOU WERE RIGHT, we picked him up at his home, as he was packing."

Drago had caught me on my new cell phone while I was sitting on the sea wall staring at the harbor. It took me a second to remember what he was talking about.

"Sorry, you picked up who?"

"Father Jim."

"Oh. Cool! What does he have to say?"

"Oh, he denies everything you've accused him of. He says you faked the video." He said it with a smile in his voice. I knew he was just baiting me; there was no way Drago didn't believe the video was genuine. "We called Anthony, and, as we suspected he would, Anthony spoke with the priest then declined to press charges."

"So. Can you hold him for trying to murder me?"

Drago sighed. "As I told you, it would be a difficult case to prove. One moment." I heard him speaking to someone in the background. "Father Jim says he wants me to charge you with assault."

"Oh, I doubt if he wants to do that. Remind him that I can now post not only his picture but video of his confession on Facebook. I'm sure I can find some of Jamieson Miller's friends on there."

I heard Drago repeat some of what I had just said to the priest. I heard only silence from the clergyman. Drago came back on. "Yes, he has wisely decided not to press charges against you. In any case, it won't matter."

"Why not?"

"I contacted the police department in Duncombe, Iowa. They are sending an officer to pick him up."

"Awesome! That was fast!"

Drago chuckled. "Mr. Connor, we are a small town police department, but even we have telephones and fax machines. The police department in Duncombe, Iowa, is also small. So small, in fact, that when I faxed Father's picture to them, they immediately knew who he was. The desk sergeant called his chief, who interrupted a judge's dinner, who signed extradition papers. It appears Father Jim's crime is well known there. There has been a warrant for his arrest for many years. And his name isn't Father Jim Lebbeus, it is Father James Thaddeus."

I laughed. "That figures."

"What?"

"Lebbaeus Thaddaeus is a name given for one of Jesus' apostles in the King James Version of the Bible. As time went on and older, more accurate manuscripts were discovered, the 'Lebbaeus' was found to be wrong and it was dropped."

"Ah, I see." I wasn't sure he saw at all, so I went on. "Thaddaeus in the Bible is the son, or possibly the brother, of an apostle named James. So it wouldn't surprise me if we found that James Thaddeus isn't his real name either. Iowa may want to find out who this guy really is, and see what other charges he's hiding from."

"I will let them know. In any case, the town of Duncombe is ecstatic. I doubt if they will care that he may have come to them on the run from some other crime, as long as they can lock him up for a long time. They were beginning to fear that he would get away because of the, the limitations of statutes?"

"Statute of Limitations. Many crimes in America cannot be pursued after a certain number of years. A lot of the pedophile priests have gotten away because the children they abused didn't press charges until they were adults."

"How odd America is. In any case, Iowa faxed us extradition papers. We had them in hand before we picked him up. We also recorded his call to Anthony."

I heard the priest squawk; apparently Drago hadn't told him that part. I just hoped Anthony hadn't said anything incriminating.

"I advised them there was no rush," Drago continued. "I can hold him here without charges and without bail for 48 hours. If the sheriff of Iowa hasn't arrived by then I will charge the Father with attempted murder pending matching his fingerprints to the liqueur bottle – as you know, my fingerprint matching process is notoriously slow – that will gain another 48 hours. But the extradition papers make it certain he will not spend another free minute on Malta."

"Well, that's good news."

"For all of us. You've made me look good. Thank you, Mr. Connor."

***

NOW THAT I DIDN'T have to look over my shoulder anymore I could concentrate on my future. Would I sell my business to Metropolitan and try to build a future with Caroline? Or should I simply be grateful for an interesting vacation and head back to the grind?

I came to a decision. I called Peter at Metropolitan, picked up the Vespa in front of the dive shop and buzzed out to Caroline's house.

CHAPTER 20

THE STORM HAD RAGED FOR nearly two weeks. Reason told Potut that, despite the ceaseless screaming of the wind and moaning of the ship, it had to be nearing an end. No storm lasted forever. He motioned Abu over.

"I want two men on deck from now on. There will soon be some sign of the storm abating. Make sure they secure themselves any way they can."

"Yes, sir. I'll take the first watch myself." Abu pointed at a nearby crewman and gestured that the man should join him on deck.

As if to prove Potut wrong, the storm seemed to increase. The noises from the tortured timbers grew louder, and the water again began rising in the bilge. Potut clung to his resolve: the storm would abate. The people would survive. He would bring about this result by sheer will if need be.

The watches continued. Every few hours two men would climb the ladder, and the two sodden, exhausted men they replaced would climb down and try to dry out.

As the darkness of the fourteenth night began, Potut thought he heard something, something different from the unending noises surrounding them. While he was pondering it, he heard an indistinct shout. Could it have been a hail from one of the sailors on deck? He began pulling the hatch cover loose.

"Land!" One of the men on deck had seen Potut's head poke above the hatch, and he shouted above the gale. "Sir, I thought I saw white water off our port bow!" Potut stared in the direction the lookout pointed, but he saw nothing. Then, unexpectedly, he felt the wind touch the left side of his face. The wind was rebounding off something out there in the dark. The air carried a smell, as well. The smell of land.

"Cast a lead." The man ran off to drop a lead line off the port bow. For the sake of his dignity, Potut tried to remain where he was and wait for the man to report. But his dignity lost the battle with his curiosity. He went to where the man was drawing the line up from the sea.

"Twenty fathoms this line, sir."

"Very good. Keep it going." Potut calmly walked back toward his cabin, forgetting until he was halfway there that he no longer had a cabin. He changed tack and walked instead to the starboard steering oar, where the other on-deck crewman was. "Take a lead-line to the starboard bow."

"Yes, sir." The man ran forward. Before long, one of the leadsmen came running. He had been unable to make himself heard over the storm.

"Fifteen fathoms this line, sir!"

"Thank you. Stick your head down the hatch and call all hands."

Almost instantly the entire crew was gathered around him. He advised them of the shoaling water and ordered four anchors laid out from the stern. The men laid-to with a will, shifting the massive wood and lead anchors the length of the deck, attaching them to anchor cables at the stern and sending them into the dark water. It was nearly midnight before the task was completed, and the leadsman was calling out "Ten fathoms! Ten fathoms this line!"

In the dark there was no way to see whether the anchors were holding, but the ship took on a different feel. The bow rose to meet the waves still pouring in from the north, but as the stern would start to lift to the wave it was snubbed by the anchors and jerked to a halt, and seawater would pour over the stern deck. Passengers who had finally become accustomed to the rolling of the ship were again thrown off balance by the new, erratic movement.

**

POTUT KNEW HIS ship, and he knew that this new, wrenching movement would almost certainly spell the death of her.

"Abu," he called.

Abu made his way to the captain. "She squirms like an eel, sir, but I think the anchors are holding. I wish we could see."

"Abu, get the skiff in the water. We are going to take the crew, the entire crew, understand? We are going to set more anchors by the bow."

"Sir?"

"The entire crew, Abu. And send me the prisoner Demetrius."

"Yes, sir."

"And Abu," the captain stopped him. "Don't bother the passengers with this information. Talk to none of the passengers except Demetrius."

The crew, fatigued as they were from wrestling with the anchors, found new energy when they were told to get the skiff in the water. While they were struggling with it, Demetrius appeared before the captain – empty handed.

"Did you forget my warning, Demetrius? When I send for you, you are only to appear before me with my box."

Demetrius' face attempted to combine innocence with sly purpose. It produced nothing more than an evil grin. "I don't believe we've reached Italy already."

Potut glared. "Italy may be right out there," he gestured to port. "But our position is no concern of yours. Go get my box immediately, and return with it or I'll have you pitched overboard."

131

"I don't think you will, Captain." He winked. "I think you're getting ready to abandon the ship and all us poor defenseless passengers, and I think you want to take your box with you." As Potut started to protest Demetrius continued, "And you can, you can! Be nice to me and you can take your box with you."

"No one has said anything about abandoning the ship."

"I have my friends among the crew. They told me what you are planning. And I'm all for it! I think it is a wonderful idea; as long as the box, and I, are on board the skiff with you when you leave."

Potut stared at him for a long moment, thinking. "Fine. You can come along. Tell none of the passengers. Get the box, and hurry it up."

"Just one more little thing, Captain. I'm sure someone as smart as yourself can imagine that once you get your box I become unnecessary. You made it clear how little you value my life. I need your word of honor, sir, before your gods, that you value me as highly as your box." Potut began to speak, but Demetrius wasn't finished. "And, and, good sir, that when I get ashore you will set me free. We can't have you chaining me to the nearest tree, or pitching me overboard, as soon as you get the box, now can we?"

That was exactly what Potut was planning to do. How much did his word mean to this worthless scum, really? Nothing. However, he still had the gods to worry about. If Paul was right and "everyone" was going to survive, that meant this little toad would somehow survive, even if Potut did throw him overboard. Toads, after all, could swim. And toads have loud voices.

"Fine, you have my word." Potut stuck out his right hand, thumb up, little finger pointing at Demetrius. Demetrius recognized the gesture as a Roman sign asking the gods for their approval on a venture. If he thought about the incongruity of an Egyptian offering a Roman sign, he said nothing about it. He simply grinned and headed below to retrieve the lead-covered box.

After assuring himself there was nothing more to do on deck, Potut went below to allay suspicions. Passengers crowded around and bombarded him with questions. He raised a hand to quiet them.

"We are in soundings, and we have laid out our four best anchors by the stern. We can but hope they will hold. Until it becomes light, there will be no way to tell what our position is."

Several of the passengers spoke at once, demanding more information. The new, jerky movement of the ship was making them wish for him to undo whatever he'd done on deck. Some of them wanted to go on deck to see for themselves what the situation was.

All Potut wanted to do was retrieve that worthless rat Demetrius, and the precious lead covered box, and get back on deck. Finally Demetrius appeared at his side, a lump under his tunic, and the two men made for the deck. Some of the passengers tried to join them. When Potut ordered them to stay below, the clamor rose nearly to rival the noise from the storm. Potut tried to quiet them.

"We are using the skiff to try to set our last anchors by the bow," He called. "This is a difficult task and will take the entire crew. Please be patient, and we will all come through this together."

"Why is that weasel being allowed on deck?" someone called.

"Before he was arrested he was a sailor, he can help." replied Potut. The questions continued, and the volume rose. Several were clinging to Potut. Demetrius disappeared.

Paul approached Julius, standing with Otho. "Sir, the crew is trying to leave in the skiff. Unless these men remain on board, you cannot be saved."

Julius didn't question how Paul knew this. "Otho," he said. "Take the guards. Stop them." When Potut tried to go on deck, Julius drew his sword and held it to the captain's throat. Potut protested his innocence, but Julius remained firm. Otho led the guards on deck, where they found the skiff tied close to the starboard side, the crew – and Demetrius – waiting on their captain. Seeing the guards advancing on them the crew grabbed boat hooks and boarding pikes to try to fight them off, but the guards plowed through them like wolves through a flock of sheep. Otho sliced through the lines holding the skiff, and the waves instantly bore it away, empty.

The crew and the guards returned below deck. No words were spoken. Abu shook his head to his master, Otho nodded to his.

Demetrius, of course, let the cat out of the bag. "The sailors tried to abandon you in the skiff!"

Instantly, many of the passengers fell screaming on the hapless crew. Otho looked at Julius, who signaled him to stop the riot. Otho and the other guards waded in and began tossing passengers aside. When a sullen order had been restored, Paul spoke up.

"Friends, there is nothing to fear. This is the fourteenth day of the storm, and the fourteenth day you have been without food. Tomorrow we will all be saved. I encourage you, one and all, to take some food and rest. Not a hair of your heads will perish." To affirm what he was saying, Paul took a hunk of dry bread, gave thanks to God, and began passing around pieces of it.

The passengers gradually calmed down and some even began to eat. It almost seemed that the noise and movement of the ship eased, as well.

Potut moved to Paul's side. "Thank you."

Paul looked curiously at the man. "Why do you thank me? I did nothing for you." He sat down next to Luke and the two men ate some bread and figs.

CHAPTER 21

SHE CAME RUSHING IN, pink-cheeked, excited, and threw her arms around me.

"David! You'll never guess what I've learned!"

"Tell me." I poured her a glass of wine and we sat at the kitchen table. She pulled the mast cap from her tote bag. I already knew most of what she was going to say, but I didn't want to burst her bubble.

"Did you take the medallion? I looked for it this morning but it wasn't there."

"It's safe."

She gave me a questioning look but didn't pursue it. She continued, turning the mast cap over in her hands.

"I picked this up from Elvis and took it to my office. I hope you don't mind." I just nodded for her to continue. I didn't want to interrupt her story. "I believe she told you it was a mast cap? It is too small for that. It is more likely a bowsprit cap, jutting out ahead of the ship. It performs the same function, but it is smaller in diameter. And because of being out in front of the ship at the end of the bowsprit they put the face of a god on it. Mast caps were larger, and less likely to be decorated." She paused to drink some of her wine and I jumped in.

"What god, could you tell?"

"Yes, that's the wonderful part. Isis! That means the ship had to be Egyptian. The grain ship Paul was on was Egyptian."

"True. But by itself, that isn't enough to prove anything." I knew she had more. I was just setting her up.

"Yes, but we also have the Myran amphora. I looked it up today, and I can date it precisely to the second half of the first century."

"Excellent! Still," I said, playing devil's advocate, "any Egyptian grain ship from the first century might well have made a stop in Myra."

"Well, not all did. When the wind was right they sailed directly from Alexandria to Italy. So, not conclusive but still, you have two pieces of evidence that your site is the real shipwreck of Paul – three, really: the Minotaur medallion indicates a stopover in Crete. That's three more than anyone has had before!"

"Well, I think we can do better."

"How can you say that?"

"I can say that," I calmly replied, "because I haven't exactly been sitting around while you've been making all these discoveries. I made one myself."

"What? What have you discovered?"

"Not yet. You promised me a dive day. Tomorrow is the day. After that, I'll tell you what I have, and we'll present our plan to your school."

***

THIS TIME DOWN, we both were working with a sense of urgency. I wanted to dig up whatever had triggered my metal detector under that Roman chain. Caroline wanted to bring up an intact amphora. And both of us felt there was something special about having the dive site to ourselves. We both knew there was enough evidence to warrant scientific study. In future, the site would undoubtedly be crawling with dozens of eager students gridding, photographing, and logging their finds.

We started with Caroline's amphora. The first one we tried to recover fell into pieces. We painstakingly recovered all the pieces we could find into a dive bag for later reassembly. The cracks must have been in it for centuries as the contents, whatever they had been, were now indistinguishable from the mud of the sea floor.

Our second attempt met with the same result. Caroline, however, spotted another amphora buried under those first two. We took the time to carefully clear all the mud away from it, so that it was sitting alone on the sea floor. I photographed it, taking close-ups wherever Caroline pointed. Then with a little jiggling it bobbed free, more or less floating, and we gently maneuvered it into a net and lifted it to the surface, by which time we were both starving.

While we ate the sandwiches Caroline had packed she slowly went over every inch of the amphora.

"Well?"

"It appears to be whole," she said. "I can't find any cracks or chips. Except for the discoloration, it looks probably like it did when it was new!"

"Markings?"

"Same as the shard I found the other day: Myra," she said. "Nothing to indicate the contents, but from Myra, we can assume it held wheat."

"Held? You don't think it has wheat in it anymore?"

"Unlikely. We won't know until we open it. But if it had even the tiniest crack, sea water would have gotten in... Don't get your hopes up. It would be extremely unusual to find a sealed amphora after all these centuries."

"Well, you notice it floated. Seems like that would mean it's still sealed."

"I love your optimism, David."

"So, if it is dry, or if we find one that is, would the contents be particularly," I almost said 'valuable' but I caught myself in time – "significant? I mean, scientifically?"

"Certainly! There is a whole field called archaeo-botany that examines plant remains found at archaeological digs. They look for clues to the diets of people living then, the crops grown, even the climate. Some believe that there were plants in Bible times with medicinal or nutritional properties that no longer exist. For example, the plant the Bible calls 'Balsam of Gilead' is extinct, but many believe it could have contained a cure for cancer. Even if that isn't true, comparing the DNA of plants from thousands of years ago with similar plants growing today helps scientists researching disease, pest and drought resistance, and genetic evolution."

"I guess we'll have to start looking for an archaeo-botanist for the project, then."

"If we find whole, dry wheat grains we won't have to look. Once word gets out they will be begging to join." I could see her mind racing, looking into the future; a future that included months, perhaps years, of study of this site, with herself in a prominent role. I just hoped there would be a role for me in that future.

"Well, we got your intact amphora. Now it's my turn. Let's head back down. I want to see what's buried under that chain."

***

"I ASSUME YOU KNOW what these are?" I placed a handful of bronze spikes and ring bolts on his desk, then added the Roman *Aureus* and the *denarii* coins to the pile.

What we'd found under the chain had made both of us acutely aware that this was now a significant archaeological site. We'd returned to the boat, and I'd gotten a tremendous hug and kiss from Caroline. So had Vito. We all knew our dive day was done.

She had gotten on her cell phone and arranged a meeting, not with her department head as I expected, but with the president of the college. I had dropped her at the beach and arranged to meet her later for a strategy session for our presentation to the president the next day, then motored back to Anthony's. Vito and I had carefully transferred the amphora to my little room in back of the shop, where we padded it with crumpled newspapers and packed it into a crate we found by the dumpster. I made a mental note to pick up the proper packaging for it as soon as possible. Then Vito had left and I made a couple calls of my own. I'd gone to a thrift store to buy a cheap suit and tie for my meetings the next day, then headed back to Caroline's.

***

138

SO NOW CAROLINE AND I were sitting in the office of the president of Saint Paul's College. He was a rotund, gray-haired man in an expensive suit that his substantial girth was testing to the limit. The plaque on his desk identified him as 'Colin Atwood, U.O.M, LL. D.'

Caroline had wanted to spill the beans to him immediately when we realized what we had, and it was only with the greatest effort that I had managed to persuade her to do this my way. I had spelled out my whole plan, and when she heard all of it, she had readily agreed. We had spent the evening making photographs and practicing my presentations. So now I sat in Atwood's office in my uncomfortable suit and tie, trying not to be nervous as I waited for him to examine the artifacts I'd just dumped on his desk.

Atwood picked up the *aureus*, laid it back down then picked up and examined one of the ring bolts. He ignored the spikes. "Where did you find these?"

"Do you recognize these items?" I countered.

"The coins are Roman, likely first century. The nautical artifacts appear to be about the same age. Did you find these here?"

"Very near here, yes. I'll..."

"You're not allowed to have these, you know. I could confiscate them." He was perfectly cast in the pompous role he'd created for himself.

"Actually, sir, I checked. It is not illegal for me to have them, and you can't confiscate them. The *government* could confiscate them if I tried to take them out of the country without paying export duty. However, my intention is not to leave with them. I want them to stay at your school, along with some other things I found."

His considerable bulk eased significantly at this news. "Well! That is most generous of you. What other pieces do you have?"

"Well, there are strings attached to my contributions, as you'll see. But..."

"What strings?"

"I think ultimately you'll find it a satisfactory bargain." Atwood's size, his manner and his office were conspiring to remind me of Nero Wolfe – that was the only reason I could think of for why I was speaking like a Shakespearean actor. "But these pieces tell a story, and I want to tell it in the right sequence."

"If you insist." He drew in half the air in the room and let it out again. "Proceed."

Now I was holding all the cards. I laid the first one on his desk. It was a photo of the bronze piece I'd been calling a mast cap. I'd brought photos rather than the actual artifacts because I'd been worried that he would, in fact, confiscate them.

"All the pieces I'm going to show you are from the same site, almost certainly from the same ship. This is a bowsprit cap. The two loops on each side were for rope handling. Pulleys, as I'm sure you know, were invented about 400 B.C. but..."

"I do know, and we don't use A.D. and B.C., we say C.E. for our Common Era, and B.C.E. for Before our Common Era." Caroline had already told me that. I had thrown it in because I knew he'd love correcting me. Once a professor always a professor.

"Sorry. So, 400 B.C.E. Good pulleys were expensive, and cheap pulleys were unreliable, so most ship owners continued to use these loops until about the third century C.E. when pulleys finally became common." I dealt my next card, a close-up of the face on the bowsprit cap.

"Isis," he said.

"Yes. Other details on the mast cap concur with its Egyptian origin. So we may have a wreck of an Egyptian ship, or at least a ship with Egyptian connections, earlier than the third century."

He didn't say anything, just nodded. I dealt my next photo onto his desk, a picture of the front of what I'd come to call the Minotaur medallion. He picked it up and squinted at the writing above the Minotaur's head, then shook his head and laid it back down.

"The Minotaur and labyrinth," he said. "I can't read the inscription."

I laid down my next photo, a close up of the word above the Minotaur on the medallion. "'Lasaia'," he read. "I'm not familiar with the name. I assume you've researched it?"

"I have." I slid over a photocopy of a page of the Bible open to Acts 27, and I took a pen from my pocket and pointed to verse eight, where I'd highlighted the name 'lasea.' "While it doesn't exist today, archaeologists have pinpointed the site, right where the Bible says it should be, on Crete. It's well attested."

Now he was getting interested. "You're telling me you found this medallion at the same site where you found remains of an Egyptian ship? Are you suggesting this might be the wreck of Saint Paul's ship? Where did you find these things? Did you document your findings?" So he wasn't just a pompous suit. He knew the details about the Pauline shipwreck.

"Yes. Ms. Ganado has been helping me treat the site properly." I played my next two cards, a photo of the complete amphora we'd pulled up, and a close-up of the Myra inscription.

"Myra?"

I went back to the photocopy of Acts 27, and pointed to part of verse five. He read the words aloud. "'We put into port at Myra in Lycia.'" He looked up at me, eagerly waiting for the next piece.

I laid down a larger photocopy of Acts 27:1 and pointed to "Julius, a centurion of the Augustus Band." He glanced at it, then looked at me expectantly. I slid over a photo of our biggest find from the previous day: a blue glass disc with a gold edge, about four inches across. The glass was molded into a face. Caroline had filled me in on it the night before.

He recognized the image immediately. "That's a bust of Augustus!" He picked up the photograph. "You found this? I must see it! Do you know what this is?"

"Yes, I do, thanks to Caroline, Ms. Ganado. This is a *phalera*, a decoration worn by Roman soldiers, similar to campaign ribbons worn by soldiers today. She also pointed out that a glass one is especially rare. But it's the inscription in the gold trim," I pointed with my pen, "that makes this one of particular interest." He looked but it was too small to read. I laid the next photo on his desk, a close-up of the inscription. His eyes lit up when he saw the wording:

CENTVRIOCOHORSIAVGVSTATHRACVM

He looked up at me in wonder.

"This is fantastic! You found this at the same site? You know what this says?" I nodded. "And you are contributing this to the college? This is amazing! It will truly put us on the map!"

"Yes, Ms. Ganado and I found this, at the same site as these

141

other things. But as I said, there are strings attached. Here's what I propose..."

CHAPTER 22

WHEN DAYLIGHT CAME the whole crew and most of the passengers braved the storm to see if land was visible.

"A beach!"

"Where are we?"

"What difference does it make?"

"We're saved!"

"Abu." The crablike man scuttled over. "I want to lighten her by the bow. Shift as much of the cargo aft as you can, then start throwing the rest overboard. When we are ready, we'll aim for that beach. Do you recognize this place?"

"Sorry, sir, no."

"Neither do I. Italy, perhaps?"

"Paul said we would land on an island."

"Yes, but he also said we would lose the ship, so he isn't right about everything. I've been to nearly every island in the Sea of Adria, and I don't recognize this. In any case, it is not as if we have other options."

The beach was less than five stadia away. Though the wind had eased a little the waves were still enormous. Potut knew that this final portion of the voyage could easily be the most dangerous. But if he could beach the ship bow-on and level, if he could keep even half the cargo on board, if the waves eased just a bit… a lot of ifs, but perhaps the gods would allow him to salvage something from this trip.

***

THE WAVES AT LEAST were cooperating. Potut had seen enough of a watery sunrise to have some sense of direction for the first time in two weeks. The beach lay off their port bow at a northwest/southeast angle. The waves coming out of the northeast had pivoted the ship partially around the anchors at her stern until she was pointing a bit west of due north. In this position the sea anchor was useless and he'd ordered it cut away. Only the steering oars lashed straight out behind had kept her head turned, as closely as possible, into the waves. His plan was to turn her the rest of the way to port and, with the bow lightened, to try to steer her gently aground just off the beach.

How far off depended on how much water they drew. Fully loaded, they would have grounded in 12 cubits of water, perhaps two stadia or more from the beach. Too far to expect anyone to swim in these waves. The more grain that went overboard, the closer they could get to the beach before they grounded. But the more grain that went overboard, the less money Potut would make from this trip.

Abu organized the crew and many of the passengers into two groups, one to start hauling the amphorae of wheat from amidships to the stern, and another to haul up on deck dozens of the forward-most amphorae and dump into the sea.

***

"HOIST AWAY!"

It was nearly midday. Potut and two crewmen had dragged the foreyard and foresail up on deck by themselves. He didn't want to take any more of the crew from the vital task of lightening the ship. The ship was now bobbing like a cork,

144

probably drawing less than eight cubits of water. Hopefully that would get them close enough to the beach for at least the strongest swimmers to survive. The rest would be in the hands of the gods.

One of the crewmen who had helped him reassemble the foreyard and sail, a tall thin Ethiopian with a permanent stoop from spending most of his life ducking the low overhead beams below decks, now stood tailed onto the starboard sheet. On the port line was the wizened elder statesman of his crew. The yard was pivoted such that the old man was standing nearly at the bow, and the Ethiopian was standing amidships. At Potut's command they hauled on their sheets, hoisting the foresail up, and it bellied out to port. At the same time, Potut and Abu cut the lashings that had held the steering oars locked amidships for most of the voyage and pushed them as far as they could toward the starboard rail. The bow began swinging to port.

"Now!" Potut cried.

Four crewmen with axes quickly chopped through the anchor cables. The freed ship responded to the draw of the foresail and spun through the rest of her turn like she was young again. The Ethiopian and the old man squared the sail, and the old ship fairly flew down the steep waves toward the beach.

CHAPTER
23

"OH DAVID, YOU DID IT!" She flung her arms around me and threatened to squeeze the life out of me as soon as we were on the sidewalk. We strolled contentedly through the late afternoon sunshine. I pulled the thrift store tie off and dropped it into a garbage can we passed. "You know, you may have to own one or two of those, Doctor Connor," she teased.

"Not if I can help it, Doctor Ganado."

I had laid out my plan for President Atwood this way:

"As you said, this archaeological site would put your college on the map. You will have respected scholars knocking down your door to visit the site, see the artifacts, and write articles and books about them."

Now he decided to get coy. "Some, that's true. However, it will sound an alarm to the minimalists, who don't like anything that tends to reinforce the Bible's accuracy."

"What do you care? The controversy will only serve to increase the visibility of your school. Furthermore, you will have so many Bible students applying to attend classes here you will have a waiting list."

"I believe you might be overstating it. Your *phalera* names the Augustus cohort, and I agree that confirms one verse in the Bible. And *'centurio'* at the beginning of the inscription would seem to indicate that this particular phalera was the special property of a centurion. However," he had gone into full classroom-lecture mode, "it doesn't mention, what was our centurion's name, Julius? The Augustus cohort was around before Paul's time and lasted for more than a century after. It had several centurions over the years." He quickly went on. "Not that I think it *likely* that a different centurion of the Augustus cohort happened to drop that phalera at the same site where you found evidence of an Egyptian grain ship. I'm simply saying what the critics will say."

I played my last card. "Remember the Minotaur medallion I showed you earlier?" He nodded. "This," I said, dropping my next-to-last photo on his desk, "is the back side of the medallion."

He read the Greek inscription, looked up at me, then read it again. "'Otho, protector of ...' My goodness!" He stopped, at a loss for words. "My goodness! I don't know who Otho is, but... 'Otho, protector of Julius.' It says "Julius"! This is from the same site, you said?"

I nodded. I could almost see him swelling as he grew in importance in his own eyes. No doubt he was imagining all the dinners, fetes, and awards banquets at which he would be guest of honor over the coming years. Not counting significant historical figures such as Caesars and kings the roster of lesser-known Bible characters whose existence has been proven from secular sources is extremely short – a couple dozen. This find would put Julius in the company of Hezekiah, Pontius Pilate, Baruch, and Simon of Cyrene. And it would make Saint Paul's College, and by extension Atwood, famous.

But he still had a major concern. "You said this is not a gift, that you wanted something for these things. We are not a wealthy college. What is your price?"

I had laid my last picture on his desk. This was an underwater shot that clearly showed the field of hundreds of amphorae strewn across the bottom. "This will be a major underwater dig, lasting months if not years. It will require a marine archaeologist, a pottery expert, an epigrapher, an archaeo-botanist, and dozens of dive-qualified students. All I want," I had said, "is to be co-director of the dig."

He'd started to speak, then stopped and thought some more. He had looked at me quizzically. "Co-director?"

"Co-director."

"Co-director with whom? Professor Ganado?"

"Co-director with Doctor Ganado."

"She hasn't yet earned her doctorate. And frankly, I know nothing about your own credentials. I can't put a," I knew he wanted to say 'a nobody' but he restrained himself, "an unaccredited person in charge of a project of this magnitude."

"I'm sure you are familiar with the concept of honorary doctorates?" I had asked.

"Saint Paul's college is not in the habit of..."

"Donald Trump has been awarded honorary doctorates from several prestigious universities in America. Bill Cosby has them, too; in some cases for doing nothing more than showing up for a commencement address."

"Neither of them..."

"I know," I'd said. "Awarding a doctorate to either of them would do nothing for the prestige of your college. I, on the other hand, will do nothing to lower your reputation, I promise you. And it won't be an empty award. I'll actually be working here. You have it within your power to award me an honorary Doctorate, perhaps Doctor of Education or Doctor of History. Those are a couple that Cosby got. In fact, since you'll be creating a course in Biblical Archaeology, you could make me the recipient of the first doctorate of that course, contingent on receiving my dissertation on the Pauline shipwreck within, say, six months?"

"It would be a thesis, not a dissertation. Dissertation is an American concept," he sniffed. "In any case, we care about education in Europe, and particularly in Malta. We don't hand out doctorates like gold stars."

"The University of Malta recently awarded Malta's most famous tenor, Joseph Calleja, an honorary doctorate of arts. And they required no thesis. He got it just for having a good voice."

He couldn't say anything to that. Compared to a degree from the University of Malta an honorary doctorate from Saint Paul's college wasn't likely to gain me any significant standing in the academic world.

"I'll look into it, but don't get your hopes up. I'm not optimistic that the board would agree to such a scheme."

"Actually," I said. "I am optimistic. The mayor is on the board of

148

your college, isn't he?" Atwood nodded. "I had breakfast with him this morning." Atwood narrowed his eyes in disbelief, but it was true. I had taken the mayor to breakfast on the pretext of offering city employees free fire extinguisher training. Since such classes were usually expensive, the mayor was happy to discuss free, particularly as the offer included me buying him breakfast. Once I had his undivided attention I had filled him in on what I'd been doing in Malta. And I did agree to the free extinguisher training.

"I showed His Honor the same photographs I just showed you. He was of the opinion that a doctorate and commensurate salary for myself and Doctor Ganado would be a small price to pay for the increase in students to the college and tourists to Saint Paul's Bay. He was especially adamant that I *not* take the same offer to the University of Malta in Valetta."

Atwood sputtered and gawped at the possibility that I might take my archaeological site down the road to the U. of M., his alma mater. In the end, he would only repeat that he would have to consult with the board, but we both knew it was just a face-saving maneuver and that the board would give me, give us, what we were asking.

***

NOW, OUT ON THE sidewalk and sans tie I took Caroline's hand as we strolled along hand in hand watching the sunset. I felt a shiver run through her and I stopped and took off my suit coat and draped it over her shoulders. I could feel what passed for winter in the Maltese air.

"This is about the same time of year as when Paul was shipwrecked," I said. "Can you imagine all those people coming out of the water, sopping wet in this temperature?"

"Yes, I often use my fireplace this time of year. You know what sounds good?" she asked. "I know a pizza place with a wood fire. It's very cozy."

"Perfect. Let's head back to the dive shop so I can get out of this monkey suit, then I'll take you to dinner." She smiled and agreed.

Someone stepped up behind us and draped an arm around my shoulder. Their other arm went around Caroline's waist, and a voice in

149

my ear said, "I have a gun in your girlfriend's side. Keep walking and she might survive the evening."

CHAPTER
24

AS THE WAVES DROVE THE ungainly ship toward the beach Abu's keen eyes picked out something directly in their path.

"Captain!" he screamed. "Rocks, right ahead!" Without waiting for an acknowledgement Abu, manning the starboard steering oar, pulled it hard to the left.

Potut also reacted instantly. But he shoved his oar hard to the right. The two oars counteracted each other, and the bow remained on a straight line for the rocky outcrop.

"Port, Abu, port! Steer to port!" yelled Potut.

Abu ducked under the oar, slipped on the wet deck but quickly regained his footing and frantically pulled the oar the other way. But the delay was costly. The ship missed a direct collision with the rocks by a few cubits but in the next moment, with a grinding crash, it jerked to a halt. The foremast cracked and toppled over the bow, stretching and snapping stays and ripping ringbolts loose from the rail. In turn, the falling foremast caught the bowsprit, with Potut's newly installed lucky Isis charm, and snapped it off. In a tangled mess, bowsprit, foresail, foremast and lines went into the sea.

Most of the passengers had been standing looking toward the unknown beach. The sudden stop threw them to the deck, some sliding quite a distance over the wet decking before they caught handholds. Otho's left hand grabbed a lifeline and in the same instant his right hand shot out and grabbed a handful of Julius' tunic.

Those below deck were equally caught off guard by the sudden stop. Amphorae, luggage and crates tore loose and slid toward the bow, plowing into passengers, carrying them along.

Potut managed to keep his feet only by holding on to the oar, but in the next instant after the crash he and Abu were buried in hundreds of tons of green water, as the waves began pulverizing the stern of the stranded ship.

Demetrius, with the captain's lead box, had been hiding in a greasy pit of a crawl space he had found, wedged under the swivel mount of the port side derrick. The violent stop had jarred him loose from his hidey-hole but worse, it had jarred his prize loose from his belt. The lead box dropped to the cargo deck. Demetrius quickly dropped down beside it but, before he could pick it up, both he and it were careening forward, driven by a large, heavy basket. Demetrius immediately recognized the Augustus crest painted on the side of it. Julius' personal effects! When he stopped sliding he tore the basket open and began digging through the clothing and equipment inside. Tossing aside clothing, soap, and a razor he finally came to something valuable: Julius' parade uniform. The breastplate held six phalerae, any one of which would net Demetrius a year's pay. He quickly stripped off his tunic and strapped the breastplate on over his bare chest, then pulled his tunic back on over it.

His lead box, meanwhile – he no longer thought of it as the captain's box – had slid through a gap where the cargo decking met the stump of the mainmast, and had fallen into the bilge. Demetrius was convinced the box was his fortune. He had fantasized about the kingly life he would live once he got away from his captors and opened the box. He was not about to give up that prize.

He ran to the hatch that had become so familiar to the bailing crew, yanked it open and dropped below the cargo deck into the stinking bilge. The freezing water had risen until there was less than a cubit of air below the underside of the cargo

152

deck. Demetrius crouched to fit into the space and, keeping his nose in the airspace he sloshed back toward the mainmast. Once there he took a breath and sank below the surface of the filthy bilge water. Groping around in the dark, his fingers scrabbled at nothing but the wood of the keel. When he could hold his breath no more, he stood up, banging his head on the underside of the cargo deck. He shook his head to clear it, turned his face up into the clear air to take a breath and dropped down again. Finally, on his third attempt, his left hand closed over the lead box. Clutching his treasure he waded back to the hatch and pulled himself up onto the cargo deck.

He arranged the box securely in his belt, scooped up a small bag that held all his worldly belongings and headed for the hatch to the main deck. As his head cleared the coaming a hand clamped over his neck and hauled him on deck.

"Here he is," said Otho. Porcius, one of the other guards, was standing there with Aelius the runaway praetorian, a manacle already attached to one wrist. Otho wrapped the other end of the chain, the end that had no manacle, around Demetrius' ankle and, as he'd done on Crete, hooked an open link through a whole link of the chain and prepared to squeeze it closed, confident that Demetrius' strength alone would never get it open.

"You can't do this!" cried Demetrius. "We'll sink like stones attached to this heavy chain! You're condemning us to death!"

"That's kind of the idea," said Porcius. He turned to Otho. "The death of these two going to cost you any sleep?"

"I'll sleep like a baby."

"Help!" Demetrius cried. "Murder! We're Roman citizens! You can't treat us this way! Help!"

Julius heard the commotion and came over. He shot an inquiring look at Otho, who explained, "They've both already shown they will escape at the first opportunity. If we let them go unchained we'll never see them again."

"I know they are trouble," Julius said, then jerked his thumb at Demetrius, "particularly this one. But Paul said his

153

God has promised to save us all; therefore I feel obligated to do my best to save Paul. And I can't save him if we kill these two. Take the chain off."

The grin from Demetrius brought Otho within an inch of disobeying his master. But old habits die hard and Otho removed the chain from Demetrius' ankle while Porcius unlocked the manacle from Aelius.

"Can you swim?" Julius addressed himself to Aelius, the praetorian.

"Yes, sir, but not well."

"Find something that will float and get yourself over the bow. Come find me when we are all on the beach." Julius turned to Demetrius, almost as an afterthought. "You, too."

Otho started to wind the chain around his waist so he'd have it with him to lock up the two prisoners once on shore, but another thought stopped him. His first priority was Julius' safety. While he was confident he could get himself ashore even with the weight of the chain, he was not as confident that he could save both himself and his master if necessary while wrapped in the chain. Reluctantly, he tossed the chain overboard.

***

THE SHIP WAS SHRIEKING like a woman in labor as the sea tore it apart. Over the noise of the rending timbers, the wind, and the surf, Paul asked Luke and Aristarchus: "Can you swim?"

Aristarchus replied with a smile, "I swim like a fish, have since I was young, though I usually stick to calmer water than this."

Luke admitted he'd never learned to swim. "I've been meaning to learn. This would seem like a good time."

"I have had some experience with shipwreck," Paul said with a small smile of his own. Aristarchus and Luke both knew Paul had been shipwrecked three times before, and on one occasion had had to cling to wreckage for a whole night and

154

nearly the whole following day before he was rescued. "A hatch cover makes a superb raft."

They got busy removing one of the forward cargo hatch covers. Luke wanted to jump into the water holding on to it, but Paul prevented him. "When you hit the water, you will go under, and it won't. Just take a deep breath and jump, feet first, bend your knees and hold your arms out. Don't try to fight going underwater. The water will be cold. Don't let it take your breath. Trust that your lungs will return you to the surface. Then look for the hatch cover."

They threw the hatch cover into the waves, then joined hands, Luke in the middle, and jumped. Paul lost his grip on Luke, but Aristarchus didn't, and all three bobbed quickly to the surface. Aristarchus swam with one arm and pulled Luke with the other until all three were holding onto the edge of the hatch cover. For a short space they were in the lee of the ship's hull. But after a few waves, the hatch cover was caught and, with its three passengers, washed rapidly toward the beach.

Demetrius had been listening and watching as Paul instructed Luke. He couldn't swim either. Unfortunately, he couldn't find a hatch cover, but he could see the foremast wreckage floating in the water in the lee of the ship. Surely that would be a good piece to hang on to. He jumped over the side, aiming for it. His hand hit it but couldn't get a grip on the smooth curved surface. He slipped off; and the breastplate on his chest, and the lead box in his belt, dragged him straight to the ocean floor.

CHAPTER 25

THE SHOCK WAS SO COMPLETE I stopped walking and my jaw dropped. "Gary?"

"Surprise! Keep walking. I'd hate to blow a hole in your pretty girlfriend."

I couldn't see a gun, but one look at Caroline's face told me he was telling the truth about having a gun pressed against her.

"But, why? I... What are you doing in Malta? Why are you threatening Caroline?" At least I had the presence of mind to keep walking down the sidewalk.

"Nice to meetcha, Caroline. She's hot, dude. Nice goin'."

I grimaced, and he noticed. "Davey, Davey, you are so uptight! What do you care if I say your lady's hot? She probably appreciates the compliment."

"David, who is this vile creature?" Caroline asked.

"Oh, he didn't tell you about me, huh? I'm his brother-in-law and business partner Gary."

"He is my brother-in-law, but he is not my business partner, he's an employee. Make that ex-employee as of now."

"Dude, don't be that way. You haven't heard my proposal yet." He turned to Caroline. "Your guy Dave, here, is a real hard worker, but he has no head for business. He doesn't understand when a great deal is staring him in the face. Let's hope he figures out that sharing his business with a new partner is better than having a dead girlfriend and no business."

"What, you think you can coerce me to sign a contract giving you half my business? That will never fly. What are we supposed to do, go back to Phoenix and act like nothing happened? Besides, any contract you force me to sign at gunpoint wouldn't be worth the paper it was written on."

"I swear, you are the most naïve guy on the planet! Do you really not get the situation you're in? I'm tellin' you, once you hear the whole plan you'll agree, gladly. Look," he said, sounding exasperated. "It looks like you're starting a brand new life here anyway. What do you care about the business?"

"My plans are none of your concern. I care about my business because it's *my* business; I built it, myself. Why would I give half of it away?"

"I didn't say anything about half. 'Partner' is sort of a figure of speech. You're going to be more of a, say, a silent partner." He turned to Caroline again. "Naïve, see what I mean? No idea what's going on around him. I've been following this guy around for days and he never saw me once." He turned back to me. "I thought you were onto me when I lost you at McDonald's the other day but I guess that was just dumb luck, like with the boat. And now here you are again today, strolling along like a hick from the sticks out on his first date, not even looking over your shoulder. Idiot!"

"But Gary, why? What's with the gun? Why –" I stopped. "*You* burned the boat?" I just couldn't imagine what had possessed Gary to fly over 6,000 miles from Phoenix to try to kill me in Malta.

He pulled me forward again. "Nice goin', Dave, you're finally beginning to catch on. Too bad it's too late." He turned the three of us so we were looking at the traffic. He waited for a large gap, then we crossed, looking for all the world like three pals walking arm in arm.

Gary continued. "Listen, I know you have questions. But I also know that in the movies the bad guy always goes into an explanation about why he did what he did, and how clever he is, when what he really should do is just pull the trigger." I tensed at that but he continued. "Relax. I'm not going to shoot either one of you unless you force me to. What you're going to do right now is call Anthony and get him to knock off early."

"Who?"

"Don't be stupid, Davey, you know who Anthony is."

I stalled for time, trying to get my head around what Gary was up to, what he was doing here, and how I could get us out of this.

"You mean Anthony at the dive shop? I know Anthony, sure, but how do you know him?"

"Where do you think I got the gun?" he said with a grin. "Dude, did you know there are more guns in Malta than any other country in Europe?" I didn't think that was true, but I didn't want to argue with him, so I just nodded. I wanted to keep him talking. Maybe I'd figure out what was going on.

Gary had always loved the sound of his own voice. "I looked on the net before I left Phoenix, how to buy an unregistered gun in Malta, got a name of a guy here. He met me when I got off the plane and for fifty bucks told me where I could buy a gun in Saint Paul's Bay: Anthony's Dive Shop. Imagine my surprise when I discovered it was the same dive shop where you were staying! I was in the process of dickering with him last week when I saw you pulling your boat up to the dock out back. He must have thought I was the rube of the century when I paid the full price he was asking, but I needed to get out of there before you saw me."

"When was this?"

"What do you care? Stop over here." He directed us to a bench with a view of the harbor, from which we could see the back of Anthony's shop across the water, the boat I'd rented docked below it. "Make the call, dude. Get Anthony to go home early."

While I dialed I tried to think of some way to alert Anthony that we were in trouble without Gary knowing what was going on, but he'd thought of that, too.

"Put it on speaker."

I put in on speaker, and we listened to it ring. Maybe he wouldn't answer.

He answered, saying something in Maltese.

"Anthony? It's David."

"David, my good friend! Tell me, how did it go with…"

I cut him off. "Anthony, the meeting with President Drago at the college went great! So great, in fact, that Caroline and I want to celebrate. It's almost closing time. Do you think you could give us some privacy at the shop? We're just going to pick up a bottle of something Drago recommended."

"Drago, you mean..."

I cut him off again. "President Drago. Yes, the meeting went well. Call him, he'll fill you in. But could you give us the shop?" I willed Anthony to read between the lines and say nothing.

There was a long pause, then, "Very good, my friend. I understand. A young woman, a bottle. Time to celebrate. I'll head home. Where are you now?"

Gary violently shook his head. "Oh, we're just strolling on the Promenade. Probably be there in – " Gary mouthed 'five,' "– five minutes or so."

"Certainly, my friend. I'll be out of here in five minutes. Have a pleasant evening, and congratulations." I hung up before he could say anything else.

"Good job, Dude, I knew you had it in you. You always were a hard worker."

"That makes one of us. So, we have five minutes. You want to explain what this is about?"

Caroline spoke up for the first time. "I think I know." We both looked at her, but she spoke to me as if Gary wasn't even there. "Your brother-in-law is obviously unemployable by any normal standard. When you became interested in a life other than your fire extinguisher business, he feared you would sell it. If he made the same impression on the new owner that he has made on me so far, his employment would end immediately."

Gary grinned. "She's a smart one, Dave." He turned to Caroline. "Close, sweetie, but no cigar. Yeah, your David is planning to sell the business to one of our competitors. I think he decided that right after he got into your pants the first time." We both started to object, but he just waved us down. "I know, I know, pure as the driven snow, I'm sure. David doesn't believe in sex outside of marriage. But when I heard 'true love' in his voice last week, I knew our Davey was finally getting some, and I knew it was gonna mess up his thinking."

Caroline spoke, very coldly. "You are vermin. David and I have grown fond of each other, but we have not shared a bed."

"Really?" That garnered a leer from Gary. "I heard Anthony

telling somebody you were sleeping on the boat, but when I blew up the boat, in the middle of the night, you weren't on it. You were sleeping with her, weren't you?"

Caroline started to speak but I stopped her. "Don't bother, he'd never believe you." To Gary: "Why did you blow up the boat if you had a gun?"

"Well, getting the gun was my first idea. But when I saw you unloading empty air tanks at Anthony's, I got to thinking about all the things that can go wrong when you're diving, and I decided it would be better to make it look like an accident. I followed you two over to that tavern on the main drag, saw you making goo-goo eyes at each other and knew you'd be there a while. So I went back to see if I could set up a believable accident on your boat. Seems someone else had it in for either you or Anthony, because when I got there, the door was busted in! So I just walked through the shop, checked out your room and the boat. I saw the two fresh dive rigs you'd set on the deck of the boat and played around with them. But you were always the level-headed one, Davey. I assume you double-checked the equipment before you dove the next day and figured out it wasn't working right." He looked at me for confirmation but I didn't say anything. He shrugged. "Anyway, no diving accident. So I just kept looking. Blowing up the boat seemed like a sure thing. Didn't count on your hormones saving you."

Just then I saw the lights go out in the dive shop.

Gary did too. He stood and pulled us up with him. "There goes Anthony. Let's go." We walked slowly along the harbor wall and watched Anthony walk away from his shop, then turn away from us and head south on the promenade. We gave him a minute then walked toward the shop.

We stopped in front of the brand new glass door that hadn't had its sign repainted yet. I tried the knob and found it locked. Anthony wasn't taking any chances.

"I know you have a key," Gary said. "Open it."

I pulled out my key and unlocked the door while Gary continued to hold the three of us together. Inside, I reached for the light switch but Gary said, 'Don't. We can see well enough." He dropped his arm from my shoulder, shifted the gun to his right hand

160

and took Caroline's arm in his left. "Dave, grab a rig," he said, gesturing with the gun toward a rack full of tanks and regulators.

"What do you need that for?"

"Just do as you're told." I went over and picked one up. I thought about swinging it at his head, but he knew what I was thinking. "Careful. Don't make me hurt your woman." He squeezed Caroline's elbow and she stifled a cry. "Carry it into the back."

The back room where I'd been staying, viewed from the doorway, wasn't much. About ten feet from side to side, maybe eight feet from the door to the back wall. It held a single bed under the wide, high window that ran across most of the back wall. A small table against the right wall had a chair under it, and its top was almost completely taken up with a microwave. A similar-sized table against the left wall held a TV. My travel bag and a rolled up sleeping bag were under the TV table. To the right as you entered was a doorway to the tiny bath, to the left was a kerosene heater.

The right wall, above the microwave, had a series of hooks screwed into it in lieu of closet space. On the left wall above the TV, as I'd automatically noticed when I stepped into the room the very first time, was a fire extinguisher.

When we were all crowded into my room, Gary directed me to set down the dive gear just inside the door and to wedge the chair under the doorknob. Gary held onto Caroline while I was doing that.

"Okay, lovebirds. It's time we corrected the gap in your relationship."

CHAPTER
26

DEMETRIUS TRIED TO REGAIN the surface, but the box and breastplate were too heavy. He was running out of air. Finally, in desperation, he pulled the lead box out of his tunic and dropped it to the sea floor. But he still couldn't pull himself up.

Now he really began to panic. He pulled his tunic off over his head and began frantically ripping at the breastplate. He managed to pull loose a couple of the phalerae but couldn't undo the buckles to remove the whole harness.

As his breath began to seep from his nostrils, a huge hand clamped onto a strap of the breastplate, and Otho began pulling him upward. Demetrius felt himself yanked completely out of his drawers, an undergarment into which he'd sewn a secret pocket where he'd stashed a handful of stolen coins and rings, and the probe he'd taken from Luke. He rose, naked but for the remains of the breastplate. After what seemed a lifetime, they broke the surface, Demetrius sputtering and choking.

"Help me! Don't let go of me!" Demetrius clawed at Otho and grabbed onto the chain around his neck. The chain snapped, and the medallion sank to the sea floor. He then tried to grab Otho's tunic, but Otho's massive fist hammered on his arms.

"Let go of me. You're fine. Drown if you want, but don't take me with you," Otho said. "Here, grab hold of this." Otho was indicating a table floating less than a cubit from Demetrius' face, but Demetrius was too panicked to see it. "Grab it!" Otho said again, shaking him. Demetrius opened his eyes and took hold of the table. "Push it toward shore, kick with your feet. Let the waves move you. Come find me when you get there. Don't make me look for you," he growled.

With that, Otho turned away and went back to where Julius and Claudia held onto a crate. With one hand Claudia held onto the crate while her other hand firmly pinned the child to the top of the crate. The baby giggled and waved when he saw Otho.

When Otho joined them, Julius let go of a tangle of rope that ran from the remains of the mast to the hulk of the ship, and a wave quickly drove the crate, and the four of them, toward the beach.

***

POTUT STOOD AT the rail near the bow, directing, urging the passengers to get over the side. Some reluctantly, others eagerly, in pairs and groups, they jumped into the water. Those who hesitated too long he mercilessly pushed over the rail. Finally, all were gone except himself and Abu.

"Go, Abu, I'll be right behind you." It was an odd relationship. Abu was old enough to be Potut's father, and he was as protective and as proud of the young man as he would have been of a son. Yet the younger man had been his captain for as long as he'd known him, and the instant obedience a seaman gives a captain was so ingrained in Abu as to be instinctive. Reluctantly, Abu abandoned his captain and jumped into the waves.

Potut took a last look around. The ship was disintegrating before his eyes. As he watched, the ship seemed to break in half and the stern was consumed by the maelstrom. He had not loved this fat old beast of a ship. It was merely a means to an end. It was overdue to be turned into firewood. But it was his.

There was a difference between captaining someone else's

163

ship and captaining one's own. The loss was far more profound. In particular, the loss of the lead box meant starting over. The government in Rome insured grain carriers, but the insurance money would only cover the ship and the grain. All the gold he had borrowed to invest in the extra cargo, and particularly the special box, was gone. His creditors would demand the insurance money, and even after handing over all of that, he would still owe. At best Potut would be on the beach, broke; at worst, he could be handed over to the jailers until the debt was paid. The jailers would sell him as a slave. If he was lucky, his skills would win him a position on a ship, but it would take years of servitude to pay the debt.

Assuming he survived the swim to shore. He stepped to the rail and dove into the water.

CHAPTER 27

GARY LET GO OF CAROLINE and pushed her across the room, swinging the gun back and forth between her and me. "Caroline, sweetie," he said. "Close the window, would you? It's kinda chilly."

She walked over, leaned across the bed and slid the window shut, Gary leering at her the whole time. When she was finished with the window Caroline started to come to me, but I carefully shook my head and she stopped. Gary was scrutinizing the kerosene heater, and I tilted my chin toward the microwave wall while I moved over toward the opposite wall. Gary saw the movement and jerked the gun.

"Don't Move!" he yelled. We both froze.

Keeping my voice calm, I said, "Okay, Gary, okay, you're in charge. What would you like us to do now?"

"You ever use this thing?" he asked, referring to the kerosene heater.

"No. Until tonight it hasn't been cold enough to need it. Besides, I don't like the smell of those things."

"Not to mention the fact," he replied, "that you know they're not safe, don't you? They're death traps."

"Okay, Gary, they aren't safe. So what?"

"Remember the Mekong Marketplace?"

A cold fist clutched my heart. How could he do something like this? How could my own brother-in-law turn out to be such a monster?

"No, Gary! There's no need for this! You want to dump me in the ocean with a weight belt tied around my ankles, okay, let's go. We can take the dive boat. But what you're planning – you'll kill Caroline! There's no need!"

"I don't understand. What is he talking about?"

She may not have known what Gary meant, but I did. I wished for all the world I could keep her in the dark, but Gary went on like I hadn't even spoken.

"The Mekong Marketplace," Gary was relishing telling the story. It wasn't enough for the slimeball to kill us, he wanted us terrified first. "It's this gook strip mall in Arizona. A family of Viets couldn't see the point of paying rent for a house when they could just put five cots in the back of their nail salon, right? The place didn't have any heat. It's Arizona; why would a store need heat? So when the nights got cold last winter, they went out and bought a kerosene heater. I guess they figured safety-conscious America wouldn't dream of selling a product that wasn't safe. So they turned it on and went to sleep. And they never woke up."

I turned to Caroline. "Gary was the one that found them. He'd gone to do their annual extinguisher inspection and found them all dead from carbon monoxide poisoning."

"Oh!"

"Yup. Rosy-cheeked, they looked so peaceful, like they were sleeping," Gary said, still grinning like a lunatic. "Which I guess they were. So, here's the scenario as I see it: You're having so much fun here in Malta you've decided to stay. You told me in a phone call about your decision, but I had a million questions about how to run your business and I showed up here, unexpected, for some direction. I didn't have a reservation at a hotel, and you being such a nice guy, allowed me to sleep in your sleeping bag in the bathroom while you and Caroline were doing the nasty in your bed."

"No one is going to believe that."

"Sure they will. Sex sells. They'll be secretly thinking about the two of you drifting away while in the afterglow of passion. They will be so focused on the heartbreaking loss of the two lovebirds, and the miracle of my survival, no one will question it."

"This miraculous survival, how do you expect to pull that off?"

I'd already figured it out, but I wanted to stall for time.

"That's what the dive rig is for. Enough questions, I'm already smelling the fumes from the heater, let's get this done." He turned to Caroline. "So sorry for the indignity, my lady, but to sell this, you'll both need to be in bed, naked. I could just put the dive rig on and wait till you pass out, but it will be a lot easier if you two just undress yourselves."

Caroline looked at me for confirmation. "I'm sorry about getting you into this," I said. I pointed to the far wall. "You can use those hooks to hang up your stuff."

"Always the neat freak." Gary pouted. "Where's the passion! Less than a month ago I brought a girl to the office for a little afternoon delight, and our clothes were all over the floor. She ripped half my buttons off!" I made a mental note to tell my sister about that if I ever got out of this.

"I doubt anyone would expect us to be ripping our clothes off with my brother-in-law in the next room," I said. I slowly unbuttoned my shirt and draped it on the fire extinguisher, palming my pen in the process.

Like me, Gary automatically noted every fire extinguisher he saw. They are red for a reason, after all. But I also knew that 'out of sight, out of mind' was as true of him as it was of everyone else. I was hoping he'd forget about the extinguisher once it was covered.

I was watching Gary out of the corner of my eye and, as I expected, he didn't want to miss a second of Caroline disrobing. Through the fabric of my shirt I twisted the pull pin in the handle of the extinguisher to break the tamper seal. As quietly as I could I drew the pin out of the handle, but I wasn't quiet enough.

"What was that?" Gary turned to me.

"What?

"Don't mess with me, I heard something!"

"You're being paranoid. You probably heard my belt buckle." I couldn't do what I needed to do with him watching me like a hawk.

Fortunately, Caroline figured out that I needed him distracted. "Is my shirt enough, or are you going to insist I take my bra off as well?" she asked disdainfully. She was holding her shirt in her right hand, gesturing toward her chest with her left.

And, as she anticipated, as soon as she said 'bra' Gary's eyes locked on to her like heat-seeking missiles. I used the distraction to jam my pen into the end of the hose on the side of the extinguisher. I knew Gary caught my movement, but he was having a hard time tearing his eyes away from Caroline's breasts. When he started to look my way to see what I was up to, Caroline's hands started working on the clasp in the middle of her bra, and Gary couldn't stand the thought of missing the show.

I pulled the hose loose from its retainer clip and pointed it at him. That much movement caught his eye, and he – and the gun – began to swivel back toward me. Too late. I mashed down the handle on top of the extinguisher.

I hadn't ever wasted the time – or the nitrogen – to do this myself, but I'd once caught Gary and one of the new guys behind the shop shooting various things out of an extinguisher hose. I never imagined I'd hit him, I only hoped to distract him long enough to get the jump on him.

The pen shot out of the hose and buried itself in Gary's shoulder.

"Owww! God!" Gary screamed and began clawing at the pen sticking out of his shoulder. I wrapped my shirt around the extinguisher handle to lock it down. The room filled with a cloud of fire retardant.

Time slowed down. Several things seemed to happen at the same instant. Gary began turning the gun toward me. I could see his knuckle turning white as he began to tighten his finger on the trigger. Enraged and losing control, his plan to make this look like a tragic accident was forgotten. At the same time, Caroline whipped her blouse over the gun barrel and tugged on it, while I launched a flying tackle toward Gary. The gun went off with an ear-shattering boom.

And Caroline fell.

CHAPTER 28

NIKANDROS WAS FREEZING. His ten-year-old nose streamed, and his ears were red. His chin was tucked as far as it would go into his heavy wool cloak, but he was still shivering. He hated being out in the storm, but the cows had wandered away, probably trying to find shelter from the storm, and his father had sent him to find them. Stupid cows. Why couldn't they have simply stayed beside the barn? His dog had already returned to the house, and Nikandros wanted only to follow the dog.

The booming of the surf caused him to pull his face out of his cloak and look up. He hadn't realized he'd come so far. Surely the cows were closer to home than this. As his eyes swept over a coastline that he knew like the back of his hand he recognized the beach where he and his friends swam in warmer weather. But Nikandros had never seen the beach looking like this.

Dozens, hundreds, of people were crawling up out of the surf, standing, shivering, huddling together. Most of them were looking off-shore. Nikandros looked where they were looking and saw a huge ship, not bobbing in the waves but sitting solidly, stuck, listing to one side, being pounded on by the massive waves. He'd never seen such a thing. He'd never seen

169

so many people on his beach. In fact, he'd never seen so many people together in one place in his life.

"Who are you?" he called. One of the men heard him and turned, then spoke to some of the others, and they all began waving frantically to Nikandros, calling out in a language he didn't understand. He stood for a moment, then dropped his cloak and ran as fast as he could to his house. His father would know what to do.

***

POTUT STOOD IN THE dying storm and did a head count. 275, plus himself. Unbelievable. As Paul had promised, every single person survived the hazardous trip from the dying ship to the beach. Most of them were wearing only a few articles of wet clothing. He noticed Julius was wearing his breastplate, but there were gaps where some of his medals were missing. Standing disconsolately, shivering uncontrollably, trying to keep Otho between himself and the wind, was a completely naked Demetrius. Potut wondered briefly what had become of the lead box.

The wind, thankfully, was beginning to fade. The rain also seemed to be letting up. The waves were still pounding at the beach, of course, and probably would be for another day or two. The ship was gone except for a piece of the bow sticking from the water at an unnatural angle, and some wreckage washing ashore.

Locals began showing up. Potut thought they would head straight for the wreckage to see what they could salvage. He had known lands where the good citizens were no better than pirates, putting up false lighthouses, creating false harbors filled with underwater hazards, and falling on their victims like jackals.

These folks were different, however. While some began building fires others handed out food, water and blankets. He watched a white-haired lady drape a blanket around naked Demetrius. Count your coins, old woman, Potut thought.

He watched a man approach Julius. Julius pointed toward Potut, and the man approached him.

"My name is Publius. I am the principal man here. We will help you in any way we can."

"Where are we?"

"Oh! Forgive me. Welcome to Malta."

Ah, Potut thought, an island. Paul had even been right about that.

CHAPTER 29

I WAS WORKING THE METAL DETECTOR over the grid sector we had designated G-7, one box to the west of the spot where the Roman manacle and the other significant artifacts had come from, putting this site in the history books. With less than half my air left, I heard the detector let out its telltale bleep. As always, my heart beat a bit faster, and I began to dig into the mud-covered bottom.

Ranged off to my left I could see three students carefully going over their assigned pieces of the grid. One was visually inspecting every square inch of her sector and photographing everything even remotely interesting with an underwater camera. Another was working a sector that had already been photographed, using a metal detector and a shovel as I was, and the third was all but invisible behind a cloud of silt he was raising as he used a three-inch diameter hose to suck all the muck from the bottom of his assigned area. I knew that every scrap of what the hose was bringing up was being examined on board the barge the school had rented to serve as our dive platform and floating workshop, and the interesting stuff would be set aside.

By the time I had gotten about a foot down in the hole I was digging I'd still found nothing. I swept it again with the metal detector. Sometimes you miss whatever triggered the detector and shovel it aside by mistake. Nope. The signal was still there, stronger than ever. Whatever I'd found must be pretty good-sized. I slowly widened the hole and dug deeper, carefully watching for things the detector would miss. When the shovel struck something solid I dropped it and let it dangle from its wrist strap and started waving the mud away with just my hands. I quickly cleared a patch and saw a square of nearly black metal about six inches wide and over a foot long. I looked at the GPS on my wrist and wrote the digits on a white plastic-coated plate, which I placed next to the square of metal. I photographed my find *in situ* then, hoping I was being as careful as Caroline would have been, I dug away the rest of the mud around it and lifted it from the hole.

It was six inches deep and very heavy. But if I was expecting treasure I was disappointed. It was just a metal bar, perhaps an ingot of copper, lead or tin. Most pictures I'd seen of ancient ingots were generally odd-shaped with rounded edges, but I hadn't studied that many pictures of ingots. I couldn't see any markings on it, but then vision wasn't very reliable underwater. I dropped it into a dive bag.

Almost as an afterthought, I swept the metal detector over the hole one more time, and was surprised to get another signal. More stuff in the same hole? I scooped a handful of mud from the bottom of the hole and sifted it through my fingers. When the silt drifted away, several coins were lying in my palm. I dropped them in the dive bag and waved the detector over the hole again. Again it beeped. By now, I was reaching in past my elbow. I came up with something slightly larger than a pencil, with thin, curving points on both ends.

When the detector told me I had finally cleaned up everything, I tied a line to the dive bag and headed to the surface.

Vito, with his ever-present grin, was waiting to help me out of my rig, and together we hauled up the heavy bag.

By now Vito knew the routine. He knew every nut and bolt of the dredge, compressor, dive equipment and boat. He was no longer relegated to collecting beer cans; he'd become a valuable diving assistant, and a quasi-official employee of the new Archaeology Department of Saint Paul's College. More importantly, he'd learned to wrap up the goodies for transport to shore and leave them alone. At the end of my shift he was always there to help me out of the water.

I showered, dressed and stepped down into the old refurbished boat Anthony had given me when I'd purchased him a new one. While I'd been showering Vito had packed the day's finds, mine and those from the students, into a large plastic case. He handed it down to me and I headed for the harbor. Anthony let me use his dock for my boat, and his parking lot for the golf cart that ferried me from dock to campus.

***

IT HAD BEEN NEARLY three months since the incident in the dive shop.

Anthony had not understood why I had insisted on referring to President Atwood as "Drago" but, thankfully, he had called Drago anyway. When he told Drago I'd said something about a bottle, Drago figured out what was up. The fingerprint on the bottle I'd left with him did not match Father Jim. The two of them, with a constable in tow, were approaching the dive shop when they heard the gunshot.

They had come running and kicked in the door to find me crouching over Caroline, holding her wadded up blouse to a bullet wound below her right breast. Gary was lying on the floor doing an imitation of a landed carp, gulping and wheezing, trying to get some air into his lungs past bronchial tubes swollen almost shut by the face-full of ammonium phosphate I'd given him. I couldn't have cared less; all my attention was on Caroline.

"Get an ambulance!" I screamed.

Anthony ran out to the front of the shop, presumably to call 112, but Drago keyed his radio and summoned help instantly. The constable crouched next to Gary and removed the gun from his hand. He looked curiously at the pen sticking out of Gary's shoulder and said something to Drago in Maltese. Drago replied in the same language, and the constable left the pen alone. He did, however, pull out handcuffs and locked them next to the shiny Breitling watch on Gary's wrist.

After what seemed like ages but was probably only a couple of minutes, an ambulance arrived and two paramedics came in. One began to hook up an oxygen tank to Gary.

"Forget about him! Help her!" I yelled.

He ignored me, but the other paramedic came over and moved me out of his way and went to work on Caroline.

174

The hours and days that followed were a blur. I wasn't allowed to ride to the hospital with Caroline, and, in fact, didn't know where it was. Anthony had insisted on driving me but he hadn't caught where they were taking her, either. Drago spoke into his radio for a bit then directed us to Saint Luke's in Valetta. By the time we got there Caroline was in surgery. The staff was reluctant to give us any information until I finally claimed I was her fiancé. Even then, they would only tell me there was some concern about her liver, and they would update me when they had more exact information.

***

GARY HAD SURVIVED, of course, although it had been close. The pen driven several inches into his left shoulder, while it had in reality been little more than a minor annoyance, had been enough to send him into shock, which complicated the asthma attack brought on by the face-full of fire retardant and nearly killed him. The day he was finally released Drago, as a favor to me, served him the divorce papers from my sister, and then promptly arrested him. He's looking at 30 years in one of the oldest prison facilities still in use in Europe, a place that has no air conditioning, heat or hot water.

However, Drago also informed me that less than half of those charged with major crimes in Malta are ever sentenced to serve any time. Most, particularly foreigners, are let off with time served plus a large fine. Nevertheless, Drago knew the system well, and he was doing everything he could to make sure Gary's "time served" before being assigned a trial date would be lengthy. He assured me he could play the system for years. And bail for a foreigner was out of the question.

***

I SOLD MY BUSINESS to Metropolitan without much haggling. The independent CPA we had brought in to establish the fair market value of my business determined that, while its value was significant based on the many profitable accounts, there was a pretty serious cash problem. It seemed Gary had been sucking the cash out of the

175

bank account for months, either blowing it at a casino or snorting it up his nose. Lesson learned: never hire your brother-in-law to handle your money.

After I got the news about my smaller-than-expected bank account I had been concerned that Atwood might have second thoughts about his proposed archaeology department being headed by someone involved in a shooting. I had visions of myself standing in the unemployment line. But I need not have worried. Atwood was a great PR man. The news of our Pauline finds had made headlines not only in the archaeological community but even in the mainstream media; anything to raise the visibility of his school. Questions, offers, applications and grants were pouring in. He had come to the hospital to give me the news, and my degree: It did in fact read 'Doctor of Biblical Archaeology,' and my future employment was assured.

***

ON ONE OF THE EARLY days of the hospital ordeal a young surgeon with dark, curly hair and a lively manner had come out to the waiting area to fill me in. He introduced himself, in a strong Italian accent, as Doctor Savonna.

"You are the man who found the Paul ship, yes? I read about you in the paper."

"Caroline and I did, yes."

"So nice to meet you." Pleasantries over, he got down to business. "You were fortunate that I was here," he said. "Normally, a critical patient would be flown to Sicily, but I had come over to do a plastic surgery and the hospital asked me to take care of this."

"How is she?"

"Ms. Ganado is resting. Removing the bullet was easy. The problem was that it nicked her liver. She lost a lot of blood. We will know more in the next few days."

"Should I donate some blood?"

He smiled. "That is up to you. There is really no need. I have found that many times blood transfusion does more harm than good."

"Really? It seems like that's all you hear about in emergencies."

He pulled a face. "Blood transfusion," he said, "dates back to

176

the time when surgeons used maggots to heal wounds and red flannel to cure pneumonia. Unfortunately, many doctors are afraid to try new things."

"But, doesn't she need the blood replaced to carry oxygen, or something? If you don't replace her lost blood, how will she survive?" I was on edge and sleep-deprived, and my tone of voice was probably not very friendly.

He patted my shoulder. "Her body knows she has lost blood," he explained patiently, "and her bone marrow is quickly creating new blood cells. I have given her a drug called Procrit that encourages that growth, and one called tranexamic acid that is very effective at stopping blood loss. I also have her breathing a mix of oxygen and nitric oxide."

"I know a little about blood gases because of my dive training, but I'm sorry, I'm not familiar with that."

"As you know, blood carries oxygen to the cells; that is why doctors always assumed it was necessary to replace lost blood quickly. However, it has recently been learned that blood uses nitric oxide to get the relatively large red blood cells into the tiniest capillaries all over the body. We're not talking," he took my wrist and turned it over, pointing to the blue line that was visible there, "about blood vessels you can see. That is just plumbing; any fluid can get through there. But to squeeze red blood cells into the microscopic spaces where the oxygen actually gets delivered, requires a dilator and lubricant: nitric oxide."

He let go of my wrist and continued. "And, as you said, nitric oxide is a gas; it begins outgassing, evaporating, from stored blood within hours after donation. You know this term, outgassing?"

"Yes, I understand outgassing."

He gave another nod and a friendly smile. "Yes, your dive training. So donated blood, having lost its nitric oxide, tends to steal nitric oxide from the patient. It also creates 'traffic jams,' clots, as the cells try to squeeze into the tight spaces where oxygen is most desperately needed to promote healing."

He went on, more seriously. "Stored blood also contains dead and dying cells, anti-coagulating agents, and other factors that I would rather not give to a patient with an injured liver. Trust me, this is the right treatment."

I looked hard at him. He was so young. Actually, he probably wasn't any younger than me; he just looked like a teenager. But he was very confident. I drew a deep breath and forced myself to relax. "Okay, I'll trust you. Was there any other damage?"

He smiled. "Just superficial. Do not forget, I am a plastic surgeon, one of the best in Italy, yes? You will barely be able to see the scar. I will have a nurse tell you when you can see Ms. Ganado." He shook my hand and walked away.

All I could do was wait.

***

I HAD TAKEN TO sleeping in a chair next to Caroline's bed. The nurse had tried to chivvy me out to the waiting room, or even out of the hospital, but I wasn't having it. I wanted to be there when Caroline woke up.

On the third or fourth day – I'd lost track – I had been awakened by something landing on my chest. I jerked upright in the uncomfortable chair, and a pillow tumbled to the floor.

"You snore." Caroline's voice was weak, but there was that wry grin. No makeup, hair unwashed, bleary-eyed, tubes running everywhere, she looked like she'd been through a war. She looked – fantastic.

"You know," I had said, "if we're going to keep sleeping together, we really should get married."

"Okay," she had said with a smile, and drifted back to sleep.

***

SHE GREETED ME WITH a kiss when I stepped ashore behind Anthony's shop. She was wearing a bikini top, shorts and sandals, with a thin shirt thrown over her shoulders to assuage Catholic Maltese sensibilities. If you looked close, you could see a very small, round scar below her right breast. I always looked close.

Vito had phoned her from the boat to let her know I was coming with the crate of our latest finds. She of course wanted to look inside immediately, but I resolutely kept it closed as we walked to the golf cart. I held the crate on my lap as she drove us back to campus, where she finally was allowed to see the haul.

The first piece that grabbed her attention was the heavy metal bar. Though I hadn't been able to see any details on the ocean floor, the strong light of the lab revealed that it held an inscription.

"This is not..." her voice faded away.

"Not what?" I asked.

She waved away the interruption. She hoisted the metal bar, struggling with it, to carry it over to her home-made camera stand. She stopped, cocked her head to one side and turned the bar end over end a couple times.

"Not what?" I asked again. "Not an inscription?"

"Not an ingot." Well, that was cryptic.

"If it's not an ingot, what is it?"

"Well, technically it is an inscription," she went on, not even hearing my question, "but not what one would expect. It is, more of a list. I think it may be Aramaic..." She wasn't really talking to me, she was talking to herself. I might as well have gone out for a hot dog.

She jumped up and grabbed a book, and began scribbling on a notepad. By now I knew her well enough to know that when she got into this mode, the best thing I could do was to stay out of her way.

I picked up the Roman manacle that had been soaking since we brought it up. I don't know why I bothered – if anything significant had become visible on it one of the students would have found it by now. I looked for markings on the one manacle, couldn't find any, and looked at the other end of the chain for some indication of what had happened to the other manacle but found nothing. Two thousand years of rust hid any clues it contained. Still, it was tantalizing to wonder whether this manacle had ever been clamped around Paul's wrist.

I went back to the case Vito had packed and pulled out the bronze pencil-sized tool. It was surprisingly free of decay. A few minutes of scrubbing with a small brush revealed why. While the curved picks on each end were bronze, the center was wrapped in gold. Looking closely at the gold revealed another, bigger surprise: the gold portion held a long inscription running down one side, and a shorter one on the other:

OUCHREIANECHOUSINOIHUGIAINONTESIATROU
LOUKANHOIATROS

I was still not fluent enough in ancient Greek to know where to supply the missing spaces, let alone to translate it; but I suspected I knew what at least part of it said. And my suspicion fit with what kind of tool it was. But I had leapt to conclusions several times in the months I'd known Caroline, and I didn't relish getting shot down again. So I just quietly set the tool where Caroline could see it whenever she managed to pull her attention away from the ingot that wasn't an ingot.

She had lit up her camera stand, and the monitor was now displaying her inscription that wasn't an inscription. I didn't read Aramaic, or even recognize it. It could have been Cambodian for all I could tell. Why had she said it wasn't an inscription? It was four short lines. Perhaps it was a poem, or a shopping list? A list of names? The more I looked at it, it actually did look more like a list of names, one above the other. The first two had lines neatly scratched through them.

She sensed I was staring at it and she began to narrate for me. "It's Aramaic. The first line reads, 'Malchijah the goldsmith.' Then 'Potut, mariner.' Those are the two names that have lines drawn through them. The next line says 'Lysas, freedman of Annius Plocamus, Vicus Tuscus.' The last line is another name, 'Lucius Domitius Ahenobarbus.' Huh." She jumped up and started scanning the bookshelves.

"'Huh?' What does 'Huh' mean? Care to elaborate?"

She didn't say anything as she ran her finger along the rows of books. Then, belatedly, she heard me.

"Oh!" She suddenly came back from the first century and acknowledged that I was still in the room. "Well, 'Malchijah' is a Jewish name, 'Potut' the mariner sounds Egyptian – I wonder if he was the captain of Paul's ship? – and the last two names are Latin. Quite a melting pot, this box."

"What box?"

"This." She was pointing at what I'd been referring to as an ingot.

"That's a box? As in, hollow, with something inside of it?" She nodded as she continued to look at book spines. She pulled one down, flipped through it and put it back, then pulled down the one next to it.

"So what are you looking for?" I asked.

"The part about '*Vicus Tuscus*.' Here it is: 'A busy thoroughfare in Rome near the temple of Castor, *Vicus Tuscus* was home to high-end shopkeepers, goldsmiths and dealers in exotic spices.' Listen." She brought the metal box over to me, held it by my ear and turned it. I heard, faintly, something like sand sliding inside of it.

"I think I get it. Your theory is that this may be full of some valuable spice; that it was consigned to this guy Potut to deliver to the Roman guy Lysas the spice dealer, and his name isn't crossed off because the box went down with the ship on Malta?"

She smiled. "Well, it could be. But it's only a theory."

"Hmm. I see a big hole in your theory," I said. "The first guy on the list is a goldsmith, the third guy is a spice dealer. What could possibly be of interest to both of them?"

She looked like she wanted to get defensive, but then she shrugged. "You're right, that doesn't make sense. What's your theory?"

"I don't have one."

"You're a big help."

"That's me." I said. "There's something else, too. Did you notice something different about the fourth name?" I asked.

"What?"

"Seriously? I spotted something you didn't?" This was too rare not to gloat about, but she had gotten used to my teasing and wouldn't be baited.

"I'm sure you are about to tell me," she said.

"All the other names," I said, "have modifiers. 'whosit the Goldsmith, so-and-so the mariner, this guy at that address. Then the last name, by itself."

"Oh, that. Well, Lysas would know automatically who Lucias was."

"That's what I was thinking. Wait, you know who Lucias was?"

181

"Certainly. So would you if you'd earned your degree the old fashioned way instead of finagling Atwood out of it," she said with a grin.

"So who was he?"

"His having three names, 'Lucius Domitius Ahenobarbus,' means he would have been an important person. He's in the history books, I'll let you look it up."

"Instead of all this guessing, why don't we just open the box and see what's inside?"

"Oh, we will, eventually. But we need to examine it carefully." She pulled an Exacto knife from a drawer and pared a small sliver of metal from the bottom of the box. It came away so easily it had to be lead. She dropped the sliver into a plastic vial. "We'll send this out for radioactive measurement," she said.

One of the many things I'd learned over the months I'd been working in our new Department of Archaeology was that raw lead has a measurable amount of radioactivity that decays at a reliable rate after it's mined. Measuring the remaining radioactivity in a lead artifact helps to date it.

She continued, "If it is in fact first century, there are several scholars of first century metallurgy who will want to see it intact before we open it."

I knew she was right, but I was disappointed. The fact that it was full of – something, made me want to know what was in it right away. Particularly if her theory was right about the three names: What spice could have been so important that it was shipped in a lead box, with the names of the handlers inscribed on it? Was it bound for Rome? Where had it originated?

"Can we X-ray it?"

"We could try, but it's lead."

"Oh, yeah."

While I was pondering this Caroline, finally, spied the slim bronze and gold tool I'd placed beside her work station. She picked it up and turned it over, then turned it again and read the inscriptions. She looked at me, openmouthed.

"You found this at the site, too?" She asked.

"Right under the box."

"Do you have any idea what this is?"

"A little. Seems to be some kind of tool, maybe. You saw the writing on it?"

"'Some kind of tool, maybe.' Very scientific, Doctor Connor. Before you give a press conference about this in the future – and believe me, David, you will be giving press conferences about this in the future – you'll need to work on your scientific mumbo jumbo. Like this: 'I can say with some certainty that this is a first century medical instrument.'"

"I'll start brushing up on that."

"You'd better. And yes, I saw the writing on it. Did you read it?"

"I could have," I said defensively, "given enough time. I was just saving it for you. See, that's the kind of thing a good husband…"

"This side says," she read with a twinkle in her eye, pointing to the long inscription, "'Those who are healthy do not need a physician.'"

Now I was the one to stand openmouthed. "Wow! You know what that is? It's a quote from Jesus, from the gospel of Luke, I think. I don't remember exactly, maybe chapter four…"

"That's not the 'Wow,'" she said.

"Are you kidding?" I said. "Of course it deserves a 'Wow!'"

"That's not the Wow." She turned the tool over. "Here's the Wow: This side reads, 'Belonging to Luke the physician.'"

Epilogue

Malchijah had a well-deserved reputation as a goldsmith. His greatest skill, however, one which he took great pains to conceal, was forgery.

He placed his latest creation into the bottom of the lead-covered cedar box he'd custom built. It nestled there securely, the highest point stopping just short of the rim of the box. The box's lid lay on the table next to it.

On the underside of the lid he'd inscribed a coded message for the recipient. On the top, he had incised his name, the name of the ship captain who had brought the order and was getting so impatient, and the name of the Roman dealer who had requested the piece. His pride then got the better of him and he added one more line: 'Lucius Domitius Ahenobarbus.' The captain wouldn't recognize the name, and Lysas would think it clever.

When the captain returned, Malchijah showed him the beautiful, jewel-encrusted object. Potut's eyes widened but he said nothing, simply gave a curt nod and the goldsmith casually picked up a small bag of seed and poured the contents over the gold object in the box.

The captain didn't ask what the seeds were for; he simply assumed they were to protect the box's fabulous contents. He couldn't know that the seed was worth more than the magnificent object in the box, that Malchijah had spent every denarius he had and more than a year of his life acquiring that small amount of seed. The room filled with a wonderful perfume as the seed poured out of the sack, and it seemed to grow darker as the seed buried the gold.

But Malchijah had miscalculated. Because of the space taken up by the gold object, the seed didn't all fit. There was about half a cupful, barely enough to fill his palm, left over. He set it aside, next to the lid.

Casually, carefully, so that the captain wouldn't see the message on the underside of the lid he picked it up, placed it on the box and quickly, expertly, sealed the seam with molten lead. Some of the

184

seed nearest the seam would be spoiled by the heat, but he worked quickly, and he knew that most of it would survive. The captain wrapped the box in a cloth, paid Malchijah, and left.

What to do with the leftover seed? Did he dare sell it? No! If the emperor were to find out, there was nowhere on earth he could hide. The value of the seed lay in its rarity. If even one kernel of it sprouted, the seed would become valueless.

But he'd paid so much for it, he couldn't simply destroy it. He dropped the handful of leftover kernels into a bowl of cold stew and placed it over the same brazier he'd used to melt his lead. He would let them cook for a while. Then he'd eat the most expensive meal of his life.

Author's note

The twenty-seventh chapter of Acts in the Bible has been described by nautical experts as one of the most accurate accounts of ancient seamanship in existence. I encourage you to read it. It was written by the physician Luke who, while no sailor, records many details that would have been missed or glossed over by someone who was not actually on the ship. I was frankly amazed that he recorded the sailors "undergirding" the ship – something sailors in the great age of sail, the 1700s and 1800s, called "frapping." Mariners differ on certain details, such as using the wind shadow of Cauda to turn the ship bow-on to the northerly gale. But it made sense to me so I used it.

The individuals named in the book of Acts were real people. Historical records tell us about Festus, Felix and Agrippa. The specific name "Julius, centurion of the Augustus band" has not so far been found carved in stone or written in any historical record other than the Bible. However, "The Augustus band" has, in fact, been found inscribed on artifacts from the first century. The blue glass phalera in the story is based on real archaeological finds. To see a picture of one go to my Facebook page, "Bible Friendly books."

Much of Paul's dialogue herein is drawn verbatim from Acts 27. There is no record that it was Julius who expressed to Paul the opinion that "Cretans are always liars, injurious wild beasts, unemployed gluttons." But Paul heard it somewhere; when he later sent Titus to Crete to help with the new congregation there, he warned him that some people held that opinion of Cretans (Titus 1:12).

No contemporary non-biblical sources have so far been found that mention Paul, Luke, or Aristarchus, but biblical manuscripts dating from the second and third centuries have been found that do include their names. Demetrius and Aelius are figments of my imagination. The Acts account says "prisoners," plural, so I decided there were three; it mentions the 'shipowner, pilot, and sailors' of the Egyptian grain ship without naming them, so I created Potut, Abu, and a crew.

Similarly, Acts 27:42 uses the word "soldiers," plural, under Julius' command who wanted to do away with the prisoners during the shipwreck, so I decided that Julius had a band of six, including Otho... who likewise came from my imagination. (Incidentally, historians also disagree as to whether a centurion of the Augustus band would have been assigned the lowly task of prisoner transport, which is why I started my tale by explaining how Julius got saddled with the task.)

The places named in the account: Caesarea, Sidon, Myra, Knidus (or Cnidus, depending on what version of the Bible you're using), Fair Havens, Lasea, Cauda, and Malta are all real. The wind that would take a sailing ship from one of these places to the next at that time of year would have to be exactly as that described in the Acts account. And the travel times all fit.

My thanks to the guys at the El Mar Dive shop in Mesa, Arizona, for tolerating my stupid questions. Their first reaction to my diving sabotage scene was, 'That would never happen.' After I pointed out to them the account on the internet of a diving instructor who died from the exact two equipment failures I describe, they got into it and helped me figure out the nefarious scheme that nearly killed David. But they warned me that some divers would still pooh-pooh the idea of any diver getting in trouble the way I described. I'm not a diver; any mistakes in the diving descriptions are on me, not El Mar.

My thanks also to pathologist John Chen for help with the details about nitric oxide and blood transfusions. As with the divers, he warned me that specific treatments vary from doctor to doctor and from patient to patient, and some doctors would violently disagree with Doctor Savonna's treatment of Caroline. I'm an even worse doctor than I am a scuba diver, so don't blame Doctor Chen for mistakes in my description of non-blood treatment of a bullet-wounded liver.

What's the gold object inside the lead box? What kind of seed is it? Hopefully, David and Caroline will have a new adventure figuring that out.

About the author

Bill K. Underwood is an author, columnist, photographer and consultant. He has been an avid Bible reader for most of his life and a student of biblical Greek for the past 30 years. You can read his columns at biblefriendlybooks.com.

He has lived in Oregon, Washington, Massachusetts, New York and Hawaii. He and his wife currently live in Arizona, where he is at work on his next book.